The Adventures of
Rupert Starbright
Book 3
THE GHOST
of
WINTER JOY

Mike DiCerto

ZUMAYA THRESHOLDS   AUSTIN TX

2013

THE GHOST OF WINTER JOY
© 2013 by Mike DiCerto
ISBN 978-1-612710-92-1
Cover art © Brad W. Foster
Cover Design © Tamian Wood

"Zumaya Thresholds" and the dodo colophon are trademarks of Zumaya Publications LLC, Austin TX, http://www.zumayapublications.com

Library of Congress Cataloging-in-Publication Data

DiCerto, Michael, 1965-
  The ghost of Winter Joy / Mike DiCerto.
       pages cm — (The adventures of Rupert Starbright ; book 3)
    ISBN 978-1-61271-111-9 (trade pbk. : alk. paper) — ISBN 978-1-61271-112-6) — ISBN 978-1-61271-113-3 (epub : alk. paper)
  I. Title.
  PZ7.D546Gh 2014
  [Fic] — dc23
                                        2013046752

To Grandparents

ALL OF THEM. ON EARTH. IN THE BEYOND.

Chapter 1

A Tinkle and a Twinkle

There was only one spot of land at No. 17 The Curving Road that Rupert Dullz didn't mind raking. It was a spot in back of his house where four large trees stood in a clump like chatty kids in his schoolyard.

Standing in this mini-forest reminded Rupert of The Garden of Dreams in Far-Myst. It was the *only* place in his boring town of Graysland that reminded him of his adventure in that wondrous, colorful land he helped to save from the terrible mind of Murkus.

That had been only six months ago, but it felt like a million years.

Rupert sat on the old tree stump that had been a mighty tree years and years before he was born. In the bark of the tallest of the four trees, the word *Folky* had been carved up way over his head in a fanciful script. He wondered for about the millionth time what *Folky* meant and who

1

had taken the time to scratch the bark with such neat and pretty writing.

He pushed his rake across the leaf-covered ground and poked the edge of the mulch pile in the corner against the old wooden fence that marked off his yard from his neighbor Mrs. Clearlynuts's.

"Rupert!" his father Polgus called. "You finished tidying up the yardback?"

The folks in Graysland weren't very clever when it came to naming things, so the yards in the back of the houses were just called yardbacks.

"Almost, Dad."

He stood and started lazily raking again. He moved the little piles of leaves he'd gathered into the big pile and looked around. *Good enough*, he decided. He used his rake to pack the old leaves down.

"Hurry up, Mister Dullz! We still have the front walk to clear!"

Rupert bit his lip and sighed hard.

"Yeah, Dad!"

Rupert hated to be called Dullz. Ever since his adventure, he had wanted everyone to call him Rupert *Starbright*. Of course, no one did. Even his best bud Squeem had doubts that Rupert had actually traveled to the magical land. The few times he had tried to share his adventure with his friends they just laughed and snickered.

He lifted the chain that hung around his neck. Once, the fish key he had Imagined had hung on it. Now, it was gone. It hadn't fallen off or gotten lost. It had simply vanished when he returned to Graysland.

He looked up at the sky, past the towering trees and into the gray clouds that blanketed the world. He did this often, hoping to see the bright and colorful bagoon of Pie O'Sky. He never did.

"Mister Dullz! This instant!" shouted his father.

Rupert flung the rake at the leaf pile in frustration. A soft *tinkle* sounded from beneath the rotting leaves. Like a little bell. It was muffled, but Rupert was certain he'd heard it. Curious, he picked up the rake and whacked the leaves again. Nothing. He tried one more time.

Tinkle.

A little smile teased up the corner of his lips, and he whacked the pile again. Once again came the mysterious sound.

Using the rake, he began digging. Clump by clump, he removed leaves and mud and tossed them aside. He banged the surface again, and this time the bell sound was a bit louder. An itsy bit clearer. Growing more curious, he dug and dug. Banged and banged. The tinkle grew louder and clearer.

Rupert was unaware of the utter mess he was making as he flung the old rotting leaves all around the yardback. He no longer heard his father's shouts. He was focused on the mystery buried under his feet.

Finally, when he was knee-deep in the hole, he tapped the ground.

Tinkle!

He grinned and knelt down and, using his hands, began to dig. He tossed fistfuls of mud up and out of the hole until finally he saw it. A twinkle of gold light winked at him. It was the same color as Pie O'Sky's rings. He took hold of the treasure and pulled it from the ground.

It was a little golden bell.

Rupert cleaned it off with his shirt and discovered little engraved moons and cat faces decorated it. He shook it and let a big old smile open on his face as its pretty, clear voice rang out. He was certain he saw a shimmer of golden light flicker across the surface of the bell, too. He rang it again.

Then, without warning, a cold gust of wind blew across the yard and sent a wicked chill up his spine. He shivered.

"What in the name of cheese are you digging for?"

Rupert looked up to see the round walrus face of his father glaring down at him.

"Dad! Look! It was buried! Isn't it cool?"

Polgus took the bell from Rupert. He examined it, and a sudden look of worry wrinkled his brow.

"Imagine that, Dad! All these years it was buried right in our own yardback!"

"Up here this instant!"

Rupert rolled his eyes and climbed out of the hole. His father looked around at the mess, one hand on his hip and the other holding the bell like a dead frog. His mouth was contorted into such a tight frown it looked like he would swallow his mustache.

"Will you please explain this mess?"

What a mess, indeed! Rupert chuckled.

"Nothing amusing, Mr. Dullz."

"I heard the bell. Under the ground. I had to free it! Isn't it great!"

"What will be great is you getting this yardback cleaned up! As for this *thing*—I will dispose of it properly."

"Why?"

"It was buried in the dirt. It should go right back where it belongs. With the worms. I've heard stories about such bells."

"What kind of stories?"

"Never you mind. Get to work."

Chapter 2

An Old and Wise Tale of Tails

Rupert, his dad Polgus, his mom Olga and his grandma Folka sat around the dining room table having their evening meal. Rupert stopped eating and played in his bowl of crispyslop soup with his spoon as he watched his grandma. She sat across from him, carefully lifting the spoon to her wrinkled lips.

"Grandma, I found this really cool bell buried in the yardback."

Folka stopped eating, and a curious look tied some of the lines in her face into knots.

"Rupert, some things are better left forgotten. Now, eat," Polgus ordered.

"What sort of a bell?" Folka asked.

"This one." Rupert held up the bell that was hidden on his lap.

"Rupert! I threw that away! Did you go digging in the trash?" Polgus shouted.

Grandma's eyes seemed to be looking far away, as if she was looking for a memory.

"Where did you find that?" she asked in a voice not much louder than a whisper.

"Buried underneath that old pile of leaves in the yardback," Rupert explained with great excitement.

"Did you ring it?" Folka whispered.

"Sure. It sounds nice." He rang it.

What little color was in Folka's face drained away. She coughed.

"What's wrong, Mother?"

"Nothing, dear. Nothing." She coughed again.

"I thought your coffus was gone, Grandma," Rupert said sadly.

"Oh, its been better thanks to that wonderful red dripsludge of yours."

"That isn't dripsludge, That's a special cure from Far-Myst."

Rupert knew it was just red water, a nasty trick played on him by Murkus. Yet, deep down, he had hoped somehow his grandma would *think* it was real medicine and it would cure her. And it had! But just for a while.

Rupert felt his father staring at him and turned to face him.

"It was, Dad! A special, magical liquid."

"Magic potions, evil bells," Polgus huffed. "If only I could keep that outrageous imagination of yours focused on schoolwork."

"How do you know the bell is evil, Dad? What's the bell for, Grandma?"

He set it gently on the table.

"The Winter Joy," Folka murmured. A little faraway smile that was at once happy and sad lit her eyes.

"Mother, never mind," Olga said.

"Dear," Folka scolded her daughter, "something spoken is not something done. Better to know and know why than not know and walk the dodo."

"You and your old sayings," Polgus muttered.

Rupert smiled. "Tell me, Grandma. Please."

"The Winter Joy was a special and wondrous holiday," she said. "On the night when the Eyes of Aranthal were in the sky over the moon, the Cat of Winter Joy would travel the land and leave gifts for all the folks in the world who had been kind to others. Who had shared and not gossiped. Who were good neighbors."

"People would decorate a special tree with trinkets." Olga smiled, too, as she recalled the details. "People made special meals and would visit all their neighbors and share the treats. Families who were poor were given extra. Songs were sung."

"What does the bell have to do with Winter Joy?"

The lines on Folka's face were like diaries full of many old tales, and she stroked them as if flipping pages on a dog-eared and dusty book.

"Everyone would ring their gildens — that's what the bells are called — on the eve of Winter Joy. In the town square the great bell — the *Gildengroat* — was rung, too, and we all would gather to hear it. Until one night…"

She stopped, and her forehead wrinkled even more. Rupert was at the edge of his seat.

"Don't stop now, Grandma!"

She went into a coughing fit, and then her smile came back.

"Anyway, often a great snowfall would cover the land like a lovely blanket. There was something in the air. An indescribable something that you could feel in your heart."

7

"Wow." Rupert sighed. "Why did people stop doing the Winter Joy stuff?"

"I guess times just changed. A law was passed that made it against the law to have leaves on your lawn and driveway and such. People started getting real fussy about things."

"Father used to talk about a man named Ensen Starkey," Olga said. "I think he may have had something to do with that."

"Rich bugger," Polgus chimed in. "Made a miser's fortune selling rakes, lucky codger. Wish my old man would have jumped on that business. You remember that Starkey fellow, Folka?"

"He's just a blur. Not sure if that tale is true. Do you remember celebrating Winter Joy as a boy, Polgus?"

"Just bits," Polgus said as a tiny smile lifted the corner of his mouth. "Was too young. But my pops told me about waking up and seeing the snow covering the trinket tree and eating the honey cakes. He used to go to the square for the bell-ringing as a boy. Wish he would have gotten a piece of that rake action!"

"What happened to the big bell?" Rupert asked.

"I'm not sure," Folka said. "My memory of the Winter Joy are so faded."

"Story is," Polgus said, "it ended up in one of those big ugly houses on Old Homes Road."

"Like that big empty house they say has ghosts?" Rupert was even more excited.

"Silly rumors," Polgus said with a chuckle.

"What about the Winter Joy Cat? Did he keep coming and bringing gifts after? Did people still put trinkets on trees and sing songs anyway? What about all the little bells?"

An odd look came over his grandmother's face, and it melted her smile to a frown. She cleared her throat.

Polgus stood up.

"Enough talk of Winter Joy. Time for dessert. Rupert, help me serve the sweet ice. And take that filthy thing off the table!"

"Yes, Rupert, enough. Help your father."

"Yes, Grandma."

"And Rupert—don't ring the bell anymore. It's old. A relic. Wouldn't want to break it."

Rupert took the bell back into his hands. It felt sturdy enough, but he just nodded and joined his father.

Chapter 3

A Jeeper and a Creeper

Rupert couldn't sleep. The whole idea of Winter Joy had really sparked his imagination. He couldn't believe that a boring place like Graysland had once had such a colorful and *unboring* holiday.

He held the bell out into a beam of moonlight that was shining in through his little window. He studied the little engraved moons and cat faces.

I wonder why Grandma asked me not to ring it?

A feeling came over him. He wanted to ring the bell again. He knew he shouldn't, but something seemed to be calling him to do it.

He studied the face of one little cat, and it came alive and roared at him like an angry lion! Startled, he flung the bell away, and it landed on his bedroom floor with a series of *tingles*.

Rupert sat frozen. Did that cat really roar at him, or was he dreaming? A chill crawled up his spine like a spider. He wondered if his grandmother had heard the sound. He slipped out of bed and knelt beside the bell.

As he reached for it, a shadow swept across his room. He shot a glance to his window. The sound of crunching leaves came from outside. Who could be out there?

Rupert tiptoed over to investigate. He peeled away the curtain and peered out, and his eyes widened.

Something raced across The Curving Road. Was it a dog? But it ran on a bunch of legs like a huge, hairy spider and had a head like a lizard's. It churned up the fallen leaves as it galloped off and vanished down the street.

That was no dog! Rupert thought. He shivered and sat on the edge of his bed. He'd hated spiders ever since one had bitten him when he was in his basement trying to find the light switch in the dark.

He looked at the little can of soil on his dresser where he had planted the pepper poet seeds he'd brought back from Far-Myst. He wished the plant would grow. Maybe it could explain the strange things that had just happened.

He looked down at the bell and decided to leave it where it was. He crawled into bed and threw the covers over his head. That night he had nightmares of big hairy spiders.

⚜⚜⚜

Rupert stood by Squeem's locker, one of dozens that lined the off-white hallway of Graysland Grammar School. The locker was a disaster; Squeem could barely open it without causing an avalanche of papers, books, clothing, old half-eaten sandwiches, rocks and a leaf or two.

Now, Rupert was trying to be patient as Squeem tried to find his jacket, balancing books and smelly articles of clothing as he dug deeper.

"Would you hurry? I want to get home so I can do homework. We have a long night ahead."

"Huh? Why? What are we doing?" Squeem juggled three large textbooks that had cascaded from the top shelf.

Rupert grinned with the excitement he was trying to keep inside and leaned closer.

"We're gonna take a walk to the creepy houses on Old Homes Road. Visit the haunted one."

"You nuts? There's ghosts and killers and rats in those houses!"

"What's there to be scared of?"

Squeem turned to him and pretended to think deeply.

"Oh, let's see…*ghosts and killers and rats.*"

"Squeem." Rupert lowered his voice. "I found this little gold bell in my yard. It was buried. Something weird about it. My grandma says it's what they used to ring in olden days on this special holiday called Winter Joy. She didn't want me to ring it. She seemed scared of it. But I did, and…"

Squeem waited for the end of the sentence then asked," "And what?"

"And I saw this thing, this big giant spider-lizard dog outside my house."

Squeem looked at him like he had sixteen noses.

"I know you think I'm nuts, but I'm dead serious. It was bizarre. And I think it had something to do with the bell. And my grandma said there used to be this giant bell in the town square that just disappeared one day. I don't know why, but I think it might be in that big haunted house."

Squeem was still studying Rupert's many noses.

"Squeem! Just don't be a dull-head. We'll sneak out and go explore that old creepy place. It'll be exciting!"

Squeem shook his head slightly then smiled.

"What are you looking at?" Rupert asked, suddenly feeling self-conscious.

"You're not the same since you met that funny guy in the balloon."

"Bagoon. And, you're right. I had this amazing adventure. It was scary, but it was just so..." He tried to find the right word but couldn't.

"What?"

"It's like when you go on an adventure, you really live. Maybe you have to have danger to appreciate what you have."

"Wow." Squeem sounded impressed. "I just wanna go home and eat some green potato soup, watch some boring TV show about leaves and go to sleep."

"Wouldn't it be more fun to go on an adventure and see if that giant bell is still in that house? Maybe there's all kinds of treasure!"

Squeem thought about it, and a tiny smile began to form on his face. Rupert nudged him and forced the smile all the way out.

"Treasure?" Squeem repeated.

Rupert nodded.

They slapped palms excitedly.

Chapter 4

Bring on the Night

Rupert sat in his easy chair in the living room with a school-book on his lap. Grandma Folka was snoring in her loung-ing chair, and his parents sat beside each other on the couch. His mother was reading a medical journal, and his father was going over some numbers on a sheet of paper.

He looked at the clock on the wall. It said one minute to nine.

"I think I'll go to bed. Kinda tired," he announced, slamming the History of Leaf Gathering Implements shut.

"Well, well! There must be two moons in the sky," Polgus said with a chuckle. "A first for everything. Go-ing to bed without a battle."

"Hey, Dad, maybe the Eyes of Aranthal are in the sky and the Winter Cat is gonna come," Rupert said with a devilish smile.

"Get to bed!" Polgus huffed, going back to his work.

Rupert smiled and kissed his mother's and grandma's cheeks and wished them goodnight. He stepped up to his father, who cracked a smile and held out his face. Rupert gave his dad a peck on the cheek, too, and headed into his room.

"Night, Dad," he called out as he closed his bedroom door.

"Good dreams, son."

❖❖❖

Rupert took a flashlamp from his dresser drawer and put it in a small black-cloth bag. He then knelt and took from under his bed an object wrapped in a faded blue T-shirt. He placed it gently on his bed and unwrapped it.

The little bell with its cat faces stared back at him, and he felt like he was falling into its gaze. Finally, though, he was able to snap his eyes away from it.

"You're a mystery." he whispered.

He rewrapped it tightly and placed it in the bag with the flashlamp. He glanced at the little clock that sat on a table beside his bed. Two minutes past nine. In twenty-eight minutes, he would squeeze out his little window and meet Squeem on the corner of The Curving Road and Hollow Tree Way.

Rupert took his pillow and shaped it under his blanket so it would look like he was asleep, in case his parents checked on him. He then sat on the edge of the bed and stared at the window.

He wondered if any more of the creatures would be wandering around. It would be much scarier to see those green eyes glowing on a pitch-black road—all the street lamps on Old Homes Avenue were broken, so it would be as dark as the Wildness of Far-Myst.

Time oozed by like dripsludge off a spoon. Rupert felt like his mind was going to explode. He wished he could use his Imaginings to speed up the clock. What was it about this little bell? Why did it make him feel so creepy? Did

15

it have something to do with the mysterious spider-thing he'd seen?

Boy, even Dream Weaver would be impressed with this mystery!

For the first time in his life, he didn't think his hometown was boring. There was actually something cool going on!

A shadow passed in front of his window, and Rupert's heart skipped a beat. He stood up and tiptoed to the curtains. He could hear the soft sound of crunching leaves just outside on his lawn. He ducked down below the sill and slowly peeked over like the moon on the horizon.

A face popped up, and two eyes were staring right at him! Rupert gasped and jumped back, falling onto his rump. He saw Squeem on the other side of the window, and he felt like a total dufus.

"Squeem, you moron!" he said, probably too loudly. He rushed to the window and lifted it fully open. "I told you to meet me on the corner of Hollow Tree!"

"I went there."

"And what are you doing here?"

"I was scared," Squeem said sheepishly. "It's creepy on that corner at night by yourself."

Rupert smiled. It probably was.

"Let me get my stuff," he said as he grabbed the black cloth bag. He handed it to Squeem and carefully crawled out. He closed the window halfway and gave Squeem a huge smile. "Let's go!"

They rushed off on quiet tiptoes down The Curving Road two blocks to Hollow Tree Way. At the corner they stopped before the massive trunk of the giant tree that stood leafless all year round and gave the path its name. Against a moonlit sky, it was like the skeleton of some huge prehistoric animal.

There was no moon this night, and the tree was just a shadow against an even more shadowy world around it. The closest streetlight was half a block behind them, and as Rupert and Squeem approached the corner, their two long shadows moved like ghosts across the pavement in front of them.

They stopped at the beginning of Hollow Tree Way and looked down the snaking street. It was dark and seemed more like a cave, as it was lined with overhanging trees and had not a single house.

"Ready?" Rupert asked.

Squeem's face was pale, but he nodded. They took out their flashlamps, turned them on and started down the gloomy path.

Chapter 5

The Pitchiest Black

Even with two flashlamps, the darkness hung around them like a wet sweater. It was like trying to cut a slab of tough porker steak with two pencils. The two boys took careful steps, watching for potholes and glowing eyes.

The trees rustled in the breeze, and there was the occasional sound of little feet scampering and the chirping of bugs and night birds. Their footsteps cracked and popped no matter how hard they tried to step silently.

"It's so dark," Squeem whispered. "How far is Old Homes Avenue?"

"Not that far," Rupert said as he jumped over a large stone in the road.

A stick cracked. The two boys froze.

"Something's up there," Squeem gasped.

"Relax. Probably just a squirrel," Rupert assured him as he waved the flashlight towards the sound. The beam barely had the energy to push the night back.

They marched on, their ears cocked and their eyes straining to see any possible danger.

There was another snap. This time it was like a gunshot.

"If that's a squirrel then it's the size of a horse!" Squeem said, grabbing Rupert's jacket sleeve.

Rupert swallowed his fear. He did not want to admit he was scared. He had learned in Far-Myst it was okay to be scared, but the fear had to controlled. You couldn't let it control you. He had to be the leader on this quest. It had been his idea and was responsible for his friend.

He stopped and reached into his bag. He carefully removed the bell wrapped in the T-shirt and held it in his hand.

"What's that?" Squeem asked.

"It's that bell I told you about."

"Why did you bring it?"

Rupert wasn't sure what to say. He shrugged. Squeem gave him a doubtful look and they trudged on. After five more minutes of walking, they came to the intersection where Old Homes Avenue began.

Most of the houses there were, well, old. And empty. They had all been built long before Rupert or even his parents were born. They all looked different, and this made them the target of insults by modern-day Grayslander adults.

"Why would you want to live in a house that's different from your neighbor's?" they said. "Those weird old houses all need to rot and be torn down and replaced by proper Graysland houses! They're the stuff of nightmares!"

Rupert and Squeem stepped up to the front gate of the first house on Old Homes Avenue. It was old Crabstick's house. Malcolm Crabstick was a hermit they would sometimes see in town buying food or leaf bags.

They stopped to listen and scan around them. It all looked so much scarier in the dark. Every little breeze was the breath of a killer. Every little crack of a twig was the approach of a deadly spider-dog creature.

"The old mansion we want is down there about half a mile," Rupert said, pointing.

"Then what?"

"Then what, what?"

"What do we do when we get to the mansion?"

That was a good question. Rupert wasn't really sure. He just felt drawn to see the place. He didn't really believe there were ghosts in the house—at least, not bad ones. And ever since he'd found the little bell and learned about Winter Joy, he'd felt a tug in his stomach. A tug of anger. How could one man ruin such a beautiful thing for so many people?

If the Gildengroat was still sitting in that old house just getting dusty and rusty, maybe it could be returned to the townsfolk. Maybe then people would want to start celebrating Winter Joy again. Maybe this would be the beginning of the end of Graysland being the most boring place ever.

"I just wanna see if it's there." he stated.

"The big bell?"

Rupert nodded.

There was another crack of a branch. Then another. Then another! Their flashlamp beams swished and slashed across and into the night, revealing nothing but trees, leaves and bushes.

Another crack—this one behind them.

"Turn off your light," Rupert whispered to Squeem and turned off his own.

"Why?"

"Just do it."

Squeem reluctantly did, and they stood silently in the pitchiest black night. Rupert slowly turned around.

He saw them. He swallowed hard and slowly began unwrapping the little bell.

"What's up?" Squeem asked.

"Just get ready to run — *forward*."

Confused, Squeem turned to look, and he saw them. Green eyes. Many green eyes.

"We're dead." he gasped.

"No," Rupert said. He kept his gaze on them as he unwrapped the bell. "Gonna see if the bell will scare —"

There was a sudden chorus of hisses, and the eyes bounded towards them like angry green bees.

"*Run!*"

Chapter 6

A Light in the Night

Rupert raced down the dark street with Squeem close behind. He was holding the bell by its waist so it was only able to make dull muffled tones. The old abandoned houses flashed by as dim blurs. Flashlamp light glinted on broken glass or faded paint on rotting wood.

Then Rupert saw it. A light. A soft yellow light floating in the air among the trees down at the far end of the road. A candle! A candle flickering in a window of the last house.

The mansion!

He shot a glance over his shoulder. Squeem was struggling to keep his legs moving. The green eyes were close behind. He never saw the thick, twisted branch lying like a frozen snake across the road.

Rupert's ankle slammed into it, and he was sent head over butt through the air and onto the hard, dusty ground. The bell flew from his grip and landed in the dark. Silently.

The flashlamp flew, too, and plopped on the road; its beam continued to glow.

Squeem tripped over Rupert and landed with a painful *oomph!* He managed to hold onto his lamp.

Rupert ignored the pain in his ankle and looked for the creatures. They stopped running and walked around him and Squeem to form a circle. Squeem crawled closer, and they sat back-to-back in a ring of glowing eyes. The breath of the dark creatures puffed in wet and steamy clouds. They hissed like snakes.

"What are we gonna do?" Squeem asked, his voice trembling with fear. "They're gonna eat us!"

Suddenly, there was the sound of approaching footsteps, and a deep voice shouted, "Begone!"

The creatures backed off a bit. Rupert turned his head and saw a tall figure approaching. The man was dressed in a black cloak with a baggy hood that covered most of his face. Just his pointy, stubbly chin and a crooked mouth peeked out.

He raised his arms high and wide and cried out again, "Begone, I say!"

Seven of the eight creatures obeyed, but the eighth remained and stared defiantly.

"I said *begone!*" the hooded man shouted for the third time, so loudly it startled the boys. His voice echoed down the road.

The spider thing lowered its head and walked off. Rupert wasn't sure if it simply disappeared into the shadows or actually vanished.

He and Squeem looked at the man.

"Thanks, mister," Squeem said.

"Who are you? Why are you on my road?" the man demanded.

Squeem's face went white, and he was too scared to reply. Rupert took a deep breath to gather his courage.

"We were just heading home."

"Home? Where? Why are you out after dark?"

"We'll just be on our way," Rupert said, getting to his feet. He stumbled a bit as the pain in his ankle flared. He helped Squeem stand then picked up his fallen flashlamp and began scanning the ground.

"What are you looking for?"

"His bell," Squeem said before Rupert could shut him up with a stern glare.

"Bell? What bell?"

"Nothing," Rupert said. "We'll be gone in a few minutes. Thanks for your help."

"Who sent you? Are you here to spy on me?"

"No." Rupert insisted. "Like I said—we were just heading home."

"Liars!" The man took a large, ancient-looking pistol from his cloak and pointed it at them. "You will come with me!"

Rupert felt like running off into the darkness. He figured if he ran zigzaggy he would be hard to hit, and he could vanish into the night like the creatures had.

But the throbbing in his ankle reminded him that would be difficult. And Squeem was frozen with fear, and he couldn't leave him behind.

"We swear, mister, we're not spies. Let me just get my thing, and we'll be gone. Never come here again." he offered in as friendly a voice as he could manage.

"No!" the man shouted. "Go! That way. Now!"

He pointed towards the last house. The one with the candle burning in the upper window.

Rupert swallowed hard and patted Squeem on the shoulder.

"Let's do what he says," he whispered.

"*Go!*"

Rupert ignored the pain in his ankle, and they started toward the mansion. The hooded man prodded them on with the barrel of the pistol.

Chapter 7

Dust and Doors

Number $1^1/_2$ Old Homes Road was bigger than Rupert had imagined it to be. It was made of stone blocks coated in big patches of moss, and it reminded him of the Wall that surrounded the Garden of Dreams in Far-Myst.

It had a dozen oval-shaped windows, most of which were sealed shut with wooden shutters. The few that were open revealed filthy glass panes — many cracked or broken. One window, at the center of the top floor, flickered with the yellow glow of a large candle.

The front yard was overgrown with shrubs, bushes and an ancient banyan tree with six thick arm-like branches that spread out from its massive trunk. When Rupert and Squeem stepped onto the property, their feet sank into a foot of dead leaves that crunched with each step. Rupert had never seen so many leaves sitting around unraked. It would have driven his father crazy!

Looming before them was a massive doorway. Pitch-black stone formed a mouth-like arch that lead to the most unboring and un-Graysland-like door he had ever seen. It was carved of thick wood and decorated with all sorts of designs.

"When we get inside, you will take seats on the sofa, and you will tell me all about this bell of yours," the man ordered.

Rupert turned the knob and pushed open the door. Its hinges squealed a warning as the soft glow of fire light poured out. He and Squeem stepped into the main living room, which was awash with flickering shadows cast by the fire that burned in the giant brick hearth. The room smelled of smoke and old moldy cheese and rotted wood. Every inch of every piece of furniture had a layer of dust.

There was a big, winding staircase that led upstairs, where a large painting of a white-haired man with a thick salt-and-pepper beard hung. There were smaller paintings all around the place of people who looked very unhappy to be having their portraits done. They all had faces like they had just swallowed a big glass of worm guts.

"Sit. On the blue sofa."

"It's dusty," Squeem complained.

Rupert nudged him.

"We're already filthy from falling down," he whispered. "Let's just sit."

Squeem shrugged and plopped onto the sofa, sending a cloud of ancient, dusty powder into the air. Rupert sank down beside him. The man sat in a fancy armchair across from them. He slowly removed the hood to reveal his face.

Rupert thought he looked like the old skeleton Mr. Bunsonburns had hanging on a stand in the science room at school, only this man had a few layers of wrinkled skin and a mop of snow-white hair that sparked with static electricity as he removed the hood. His pointy chin was like a cactus with spikes of gray stubble. His eyes were icy blue, and they radiated frigid cold.

He studied the boys for a moment as the fire snapped and crackled in the fireplace.

Rupert decided to break the silence.

"So, what's your name?"

"I will ask the questions," the man growled. "Tell me about this bell."

"What bell?" Rupert replied.

"Your chum here said you lost your bell. Those creatures are not regular residents of Graysland. Strange happenings."

"What kind of strange happenings? Nothing strange ever happens in Graysland. Just a dumb ol' boring place."

The man smirked and nodded.

"Boring, indeed. How I like it. But the last few days those devilish spiders have been round and about. Not very typical for Graysland, right?"

"Maybe they're just passing through?" Rupert offered.

The man smiled wide, revealing a mouth full of brown and broken teeth. One front tooth was capped with gold, and another had a large emerald fastened on it.

"I would not underestimate the creatures or their wants. Now..." he said, leaning forward, his smile twisting into a horrible frown. "The bell. Where did you find it?"

Rupert locked gazes with the man and held it firm. Or perhaps he was trapped in his glare? He put his mind to work.

He had known from the start there was something odd about the bell. He could tell by the chills it had given him, and by the way his father and grandmother had reacted to it. Even though it was pretty and unusual, there was something...ugly...about it. He desperately wanted to know its story.

"I found it in my yardback a few days ago."

The man's face grew more animated.

"What did it look like?"

"Gold, with little cat faces and moons on it. Wooden handle."

The man sat back in his chair and nodded and mumbled to himself. Finally, he looked at Rupert again.

"Did you ring it?"

Rupert could still hear his grandmother asking the same question. He nodded.

The man closed his eyes a moment and mumbled more. Rupert glanced at Squeem, and the man opened his eyes and glared at them.

"It was you who released them demons, then. It was you carelessly ringing that bell!"

"I just found it. I had no idea..."

The man jumped to his feet.

"Where did you lose it?" he shouted.

Rupert was growing even more nervous. He pointed toward the door.

"Just outside. I tripped, and it fell from my hand. It landed on something soft 'cause it didn't make a sound."

The man grabbed the flashlamp from Rupert's hand. He pointed the pistol again.

"Get up. Both of you."

They stood up. The man waved the gun toward the staircase.

"Up. Go upstairs."

"Why?" Rupert asked.

"I have to find that bell. Can't have you two nosing around."

"We can help you find it," Rupert suggested.

"Yeah!" Squeem agreed.

"*No.* Up the steps."

Rupert and Squeem walked to the wide, winding staircase and climbed. The man was only a step or so behind, prodding them to hurry. Rupert's ankle still ached.

When they reached the top, the man ordered Squeem into a small room with a blue door. He slammed it shut and locked it. Rupert was told to enter the room just to the left of it with a green door. It, too, was locked.

Rupert pressed his ear against the door and listened as the man descended the steps. He had to think fast. He scanned the room, which was about the size of his own bedroom.

There were a few pieces of furniture covered with large yellowing sheets. A window with closed shutters was on the far wall. A small oil lamp flickered with soft, yellow fire and made the shadows sway to and fro.

Rupert tugged and yanked open the shutters with a bit of difficulty. The filthy window overlooked the side yard of the house, which was overgrown with thick vines that snaked around leafless trees. He could hear rummaging, and the crunch of feet through dry leaves.

Then, a flashlamp beamed across the ground, and the man appeared, searching in the leaves. For the bell. But why?

What was the truth about this mysterious little bell? He had to get it back and bury it again. But would that make a difference? He knew one thing for sure—nothing was going to happen if he stayed locked in this room. He had to get out.

He turned to the wall his room shared with Squeem's and knocked on it. After a few seconds, Squeen returned the knock.

"Squeem, can you hear me?"

"Yeah. We gotta get outta here!" Squeem's voice was shaky.

"Just relax. I'll..." A powerful word popped into his head. "I'll Imagine something."

Rupert smiled to himself. Since he'd returned from Far-Myst, his Imagining ability had left him. No matter how hard he tried, he could not use the wonderful power he had wielded almost at will in that colorful land. His fish key had disappeared, and the his pepper poet seeds had failed to sprout.

Yet now, he suddenly felt a surge of confidence. He closed his eyes and tried to quiet his busy mind. He tried to envision a key. Heck, he'd done it before! His fish key popped into his mind. He felt for the chain around his neck.

Rats. Nothing.

He suddenly noticed a light on the wall. It wasn't the deep yellow from the lantern. This light was bluish-white and outshone the little flame.

The moon must be peeking through the clouds, Rupert thought.

He closed his eyes again. His mind jumped back to the night when Pie O'Sky had floated over The Curving Road and presented the door to Far-Myst. He could feel the sadness he always felt when the moonlight entered his bedroom and reminded him he would never go again to the magic world.

The shadow passed, and there he was — Pie O'Sky in his Grand Bagoon! A wave of happiness washed over Rupert. He opened his eyes, and the moonlight grew brighter. Then it flickered.

It flickered!

Rupert raced to the window and look at the sky. The moon was smiling through a break in the clouds. Something else was floating before the clouds.

The bagoon! The great big colorful Grand Bagoon of Pie O'Sky had returned!

Rupert's smile stretched his cheeks so much it almost hurt. He laughed out loud and his mouth formed the name: *Pie O'Sky.*

Then something even wilder happened. On the dirty, dusty window, the color of the moonlight changed from bluish-white to a mix of reds and yellows and greens and purples. A purple-bearded face formed, projected onto the glass as if it had become the screen of a TV set.

"Pie O'Sky!" Rupert shouted in joy.

The face smiled and then spoke. The words did not fill Rupert's ears but somehow, magically, popped into his mind.

Tell me about your key.

Rupert's mind raced. A key? Did he mean the fish key or a new key? Was there a door to some magical new place or back to Far-Myst, or was it a key to open the door to the room that imprisoned him?

He wasn't sure. He set his brain thinking. He looked at the door to the room. There was no keyhole! He turned to Pie O'Sky's face.

"There isn't a keyhole!" he shouted.

The colorful face smiled wider. The eyes looked downward, and Rupert followed their gaze. Then he saw it.

A door. A red door with a frame sat on a bed of leaves just inside a small grove of trees. The man who was keeping them prisoner was not in sight.

Rupert had two problems. First, he had to Imagine a key. Second, he couldn't get to the door he needed the key to open.

He studied the windows. There was a rusty latch. He pried at it and, after some struggle, managed to flip it open. He gripped the bottom of the window and lifted. It was stuck from years of weather and dirt.

He tried again. Not an eensy-teensy, itty-bitty, tiny part of an inch did it move.

Maybe the window had simply forgotten how to open? People forgot things. Why not windows? He'd used to be able to whistle, but then he hadn't done it in so long that he'd forgotten how. It became really hard, like when he'd first tried to do it.

"Window," he said aloud, "you need to open. You need to let me lift you up so I can get out!"

"Who are you talking to?" Squeem shouted from the next room.

"I'm trying to open the window!" Rupert explained.

"Use your hands not your mouth, dumbskull!"

Rupert tried again. He strained and struggled and cursed under his breath and exhaled hard and made all sorts of funny sounds.

Nothing.

Then he remembered something else. When he was able to whistle, it had been easy. Real easy. He didn't even have to think about it, he just did it. No struggle.

He took a deep breath, and using just two fingers, he lifted the window.

Up it went! Not a squeak or a squeal, only the sound of the wind outside and insects filled his ears. He leaned his head out and scanned the grounds below. The man was gone, and the door sat waiting.

Up in the sky, Pie O'Sky's bagoon drifted, silhouetted against the moon, its magic colors just shades of black and gray.

Rupert saw there was a ledge just below the window that seemed to run around the entire house. The sound of footsteps sounded from beyond the door. He knew he had to act fast. He pounded on the wall.

"Squeem! Put something against the door. I have an idea!"

"Like what?"

Rupert had no time to answer Squeem's questions.

"Anything! A chair or table. Fast!"

He grabbed one of the sheet-covered chairs in his own room and propped it under the doorknob. Just in time. The knob turned, but the man couldn't open it.

"What is going on in there?" he yelled.

Rupert ignored him and ran back to the window. The man began pounding on the door, and the knob shook frantically. Rupert took a deep breath and climbed out onto the ledge.

Chapter 8

Starry, Starry Key

Rupert stepped carefully along the ledge, clinging to the thick vines of ivy that grew on the walls. He came to the window of Squeem's room and knocked hard on the glass; he hoped Squeem had secured the door. The inner shutters were open and he could see the dim light of a lantern through the mucky glass.

Squeem finally appeared.

"Did you block the door?" Rupert asked.

Squeem nodded and tried to open the window. Like the one in Rupert's room, it had forgotten how.

"I can't open it!" Squeem was scared.

"Relax and just lift it. Don't force it," Rupert explained. The pounding on the door of his room sounded angrier.

Again Squeem tried. Nothing. The window didn't have a lip on the outside so there was no way for Rupert to help.

The pounding switched from the door to Rupert's room to Squeem's. Squeem's face twisted with fear.

"He's trying to get in!"

"Try again! Lift!"

Squeem strained and struggled. Rupert knew there was no time to explain about the bad memories of windows. Drastic measures had to be taken.

He pressed his forehead against the glass and scanned the inside of the room until he spotted a chair.

"Grab that chair behind you and throw it through the window!"

"You mean break it?" Squeem smiled at the idea.

"Yes!"

There was a squeal of wood scraping against wood. The man was slowly pushing the door open despite the large table trying to hold it shut. He would be in soon.

"Hurry!" Rupert yelled.

Squeem grabbed the chair and lifted it.

"Wait! Let me get out of the way!" Rupert moved to one side of the window so he wouldn't have glass rain all over him.

Squeem let the chair fly. All Rupert heard was a thud. There was no ring of even a single shard of broken glass.

"It didn't work!" Squeem shouted.

Hanging on to the ivy, Rupert leaned over so he could peek through the window. The man was growling like a wild animal as he inched open the door.

"Try again! Harder!" he screamed.

Squeem picked the chair up and let it fly again.

Thud.

The door burst open, the table flew across the floor and slammed into the desk where the lantern sat. The lantern toppled, and flaming oil poured over the sheets that covered the furniture. More flames exploded.

The man howled as waves of heat chased him back. Squeem stood petrified.

Rupert gazed through the window in horror. Squeem just stared at the growing inferno.

"Squeem! The window!!"

His friend didn't move.

Rupert's mind went into overdrive, and he looked all around for something to use. He recalled that a stone he had stepped on had felt loose. He went back to it and tested it with his foot. It *was* loose.

He tightened his grip on the thick ivy with one hand, reached down, and used the tips of his fingers on the other hand to pry the stone free from the ancient mortar. It was heavier than he'd expected.

The ledge was so narrow he was afraid if he used both hands he would end up splattered in the piles of leaves two stories below. The glow of the growing fire flickered on the ledge and the nearby trees and reminded him to hurry.

The vine he was holding pulled free from the wall, and he nearly fell off the ledge. His heart pounded, but he clung harder as he continued to work on the stone. Closing his eyes, he Imagined he was as strong as one of the Wall People in Far-Myst.

Stone rasped on stone, and he summoned every ounce of energy. He took a deep breath, and as he exhaled the stone was freed! A rush of hope filled him. He returned to the window and flung it.

A cascade of glass and broken window frame rained down around him. Flames danced wildly as the breeze rushed into the room. Squeem had to move fast, or the fire would engulf him, too.

"Come on!" Rupert screamed.

Squeem still just stood, staring.

"Squeem, *come on*!"

Finally, Squeem snapped back to attention and rushed to the window. Rupert helped him onto the ledge. They stepped carefully around to the side of the house as fast as they could to a thick drain pipe descending from the roof. One after the other, they shimmied down. They could smell the smoke and see the glow of flames.

"You okay?" Rupert asked.

Squeem was breathing hard.

"Yeah. Let's go!"

They raced off toward Old Homes Road, but Rupert caught a glimpse of the red door and stopped. He looked skyward, where Pie O'Sky's bagoon was fading into the distance.

"Rupert," Squeem pleaded, "come on before he comes after us!"

"No. The door."

"I'm going home, Rupert. Come on! Please!"

"Go. Go. Run as fast as you can. Unless you want to come with me?"

They stood staring at each other for a long moment. The front door of the mansion slammed open. Squeem's eyes bugged.

"Thanks, Rupert. You saved my life."

"No problem." Rupert smiled. "Now go!"

Squeem took off. The man shouted as he dashed from his burning house.

Rupert crossed the lawn to the red door. He closed his eyes and in his mind's eye the two stars of Winter Joy shined bright and silver in the sky.

Suddenly, he felt a spark in his Imaginings — a spark that hadn't glowed in a long time. He saw a starry key falling from the sky with a glittering tail like a meteor.

"You!"

Rupert opened his eyes. The man stood at the corner of the house about fifty feet away. He hadn't chased after Squeem.

"I have you now!" the man growled as he limped towards Rupert. The gun was in his hand.

Rupert's heart was beating fast, and he felt heat in his chest. There was an odd golden glow showing through his shirt. It wasn't from the moon, and it wasn't from the fire.

He grabbed his chest and felt it. Something was there on the chain.

He took it out and looked at it. It was the fish key, glittering with stars!

The man was closer, and he raised the gun toward Rupert. A voice sounded in Rupert's mind. The voice of Pie O'Sky.

The stars in the key are the stars in your mind. If you may and if you might, enter the door, Rupert Starbright.

The man's shouts suddenly became muffled and the smell of smoke, the flicker of firelight, and, in fact, everything around him began to dissolve like sugar in water. Rupert calmly took the starry key from the chain and put it into the golden keyhole on the door. With a click, the lock opened, and he stepped through.

Chapter 9

Not in Graysland Anymore?

Rupert looked around and, for a second, panicked. This side of the door looked the same as the other side.

He was in a grove of trees, and there was the smell of smoke in the air. He looked around frantically. There was no mansion. No man with a gun. But he could hear the sound of approaching sirens.

He walked a few feet and saw a dirt road lit by a few street lamps that had flames where normally light bulbs would be.

I don't remember seeing those in Graysland. Where am I? he wondered.

The sirens grew louder, and now he could also hear a cloppity-cloppity sound of horse's hooves.

Then he saw them. Racing down the dirt road was a team of brown-and-white horses pulling a large wagon. As it sped by him, he read the words printed on its side:

Gracelandville Fire Department. Four firemen sat in the rear of the wagon while a fifth drove the team.

Rupert watched it travel down the path toward the distant firelight.

Gracelandville? Horses pulling a fire engine?

He jogged after them. There were no houses along the path, just trees and shrubs. He began to hear people, some shouting. There was a small structure up in flames.

It wasn't the mansion on Old House Avenue. It was a smaller building that was open at the front and made of wood; he could tell it was a barn. A man wearing blue overalls led a cow away from the flames as the firemen began pumping water into the growing inferno.

A cozy-looking house sat a few yards from the barn. It was painted bright red, a happy shade he had never seen in Graysland.

He crept closer and hid behind a large tree to watch. Nothing ever seemed to burn in Graysland — well, other than the gigantic piles of leaves that were burned in the steam plant to make electricity. He hadn't seen firemen at work since the time Mr. Nicenough got stuck in his tree trying to rescue his cat. The cat had climbed down by itself, leaving the old guy stuck up on a high branch while it sat at the bottom of the trunk as if trying to guide its person down.

Rupert's mind jumped back to the big mansion on Old Homes Avenue. That had been burning. He could just picture all the firetrucks, and the curious neighbors peeking out windows and doors wondering what was going on. He hoped Squeem was back in his bed by now, looking out his own window and pretending to not have a clue what the fuss was about.

He was sure his own father would be standing out on the lawn, watching the trucks zoom by and wondering if he would have any extra orders for coffins to fill when he got to work the next morning at Graysland Coffinmakers Place.

Rupert hoped not.

"Hey, did you start that fire?"

The voice came from above him, snapping him from his thoughts and sending his heart leaping into his throat. He looked up to see a kid about his age sitting on a thick branch, tattered shoes dangling just a few inches from Rupert's head.

"No!" he said. "Did you?"

The kid jumped from the branch. He was shorter than Rupert but glared at him with a sneer on his dirty, greasy face. His green shirt was covered in poorly sewn patches, and his blue shorts had threads hanging from the hems. He also had a bruise on his right cheek and a blackened left eye. He seemed to be sizing Rupert up.

"I ain't never seen the likes of you around here. Funny-looking rich-boy clothes." he said and spat on the ground, just missing Rupert's shoe.

Rupert frowned as he watched the little pool of spit soak into the dry soil.

"I'm not rich. Just regular. I live down the road. I think. Is this Graysland?"

The kid's expression went through a series of humorous changes until he chuckled in a surprisingly high voice.

"You batty? I bet you *did* start that fire. One o' them pyro kook-a-jobs that like watching things burn. I oughta run and get a cop."

"I did *not* start it! I just got here. I came through…" Rupert stopped and decided to not reveal the story of Pie O'Sky's door. Where is Pie O'Sky? "I was walking along and got lost. Heard the fire trucks. How come they're pulled by horses?"

"What are they gonna get pulled by? Chickens?" the kid said with another high-pitched chuckle. "You *are* a kook-a-job."

42

A wash of thick white smoke blew over them as the fire was brought under control. Rupert coughed. The kid grabbed him by the arm and pulled him a few feet away.

"Why are you wandrin' around so late?" he demanded. "Shouldn't you rich boys be sleeping so you can go to your fancy schools in the a.m.?"

Rupert was growing annoyed at the kid's accusations.

"I said I ain't rich! And I ain't a kook-a-job. I'm just lost. What's the name of this road?"

"This road ain't got no name. What street you live on?"

"Curving Road."

"I knew you were rich! That's that brand new street they're building with them fancy houses. Just a step from all them big mansions."

Rupert smiled. "Old Homes Avenue?"

"No. Big Oaks Way."

Rupert lost his smile.

"Can you tell me how to get back to Curving?"

The kid grabbed him by the arm again and led him off. They hurried past the burned-out barn and the fire trucks and horses. They then crossed a pebbly stretch to a wider avenue lined with small wooden houses and tall pines and oaks.

Rupert heard a familiar crunch under his feet, and when he looked, he discovered there were leaves everywhere—lying in thick layers on lawns, scattered across the poorly paved road, and even stuck on the roofs of the houses.

"Don't you rake leaves around here?" he asked the boy.

"Only when we wanna make big piles to jump in."

The kid guided Rupert past a storefront from which loud piano music poured out along with laughter and chatter. Then, they stepped onto a sidewalk past a series of short

43

brick buildings illuminated by the soft flickering of the streetlights.

Rupert took it all in and tried to find something — anything — that looked familiar.

Finally, they stopped on a corner where the streetlights ended. A road, wide and curving, was before them. It was lined with the wooden frames of houses-to-be that all were pretty much alike. Large stacks of bricks and mounds of dirt stood beside the road, which was paved with gray cobblestones.

Rupert studied it a moment.

"This looks familiar," he finally said.

"Not sure how you live here, " the kid said. "None of the houses is finished."

"This is The Curving Road?"

"Read the sign, dummy."

The kid pointed at a rectangular sign attached to a wooden pole. It read *Magpie Song Boulevard*.

"Pretty fancy-shmancy name."

"This ain't The Curving Road," Rupert said with disappointment.

"It curves, but it would be pretty boring to call it Curving Road, don't you think?"

Suddenly, the kid's eyes moved to look over Rupert's shoulder and widened.

"Hey! You! Get ova here, you little bugger!"

Rupert turned to see a round-faced man dressed in brown pants and a blue shirt. The man's droopy mustache reminded him of his father's. It was clear the man was not happy.

"I saw you steal those birds from my shop!" he shouted as he jogged, with some effort, towards them. He was panting for breath after just a few steps.

"Follow me!" the kid said as he took off down the dark and cobblestoned Curving Road.

Rupert followed him past the partially built homes and piles of construction materials. They ducked down a narrow street and stopped behind a tall stack of lumber. The round-faced man was nowhere to be seen.

"That ol' poop can't run a faucet." The kid laughed. "Hey, you wanna see the birds?"

Rupert didn't reply. He was staring at a clump of trees not far away. The kid followed his gaze then studied him with a smirk.

"What are you staring at?"

"These five trees. They look familiar," Rupert mumbled.

He continued down the narrow street then across a grassy field and stopped amidst the trees. He tilted his head back as he touched the trunk of the largest of the group. The other four were all about the same size, and they surrounded the fifth in a sort of square.

Rupert strolled around them, scanning their bark up, down and around. Finally, he froze. There, at eye level on the tallest tree, was the name *Folky*, freshly scratched in pretty script.

He had no more doubt where he was. *When* he was, was a completely different question.

Chapter 10

Back at the Start

"This big tree is just a stump where I live." Rupert said, tapping the big center tree with his palm. "And that word *Folky* is way up high. Always wondered what it meant."

"It means me," the kid said, tapping his chest.

"You?"

"Yeah." Folky sounded defensive. "Have a problem with my name? What's yours?"

"Rupert."

"Rich kid name," Folky said with a sneer.

"It is not!" Rupert was getting annoyed at being called a rich kid. He studied Folky's face. There was something familiar about him, especially his eyes. "Why did you carve your name in the tree?"

Folky shrugged. "Why not?"

Rupert studied the writing and shook his head in amazement then mumbled, "How can this tree be the same one that's in my yardback?"

He paced and continued talking to himself, trying to work it out.

"I went through Pie O'Sky's door. There was that fire truck pulled by horses. This tree looks the same, but it's shorter." Then a thought lifted his eyebrows. "*Younger*." He turned to Folky. "What's the date?"

"What kind o' kid are you? It's three days before Winter Joy!"

Rupert mouthed the words *Winter Joy*. His eyes widened, and he understood something amazing.

I'm back in time. Back in old Graysland. That's where Pie O'Sky sent me!

He decided it best to keep this fact from Folky, who already thought he was crazy.

Rupert looked around in amazement. This was his own yardback. Well, it was going to be, sometime in the future. His house wasn't finished, but the foundation was down; and the start of its wooden frame was going up. He could see where his bedroom would be. Where his living room was.

He thought of his parents. Did they know he was gone? What about Squeem? Did he get home okay? And there was the fire on Old Homes Avenue in that strange man's house. Would the firemen find the bell?

"The bell!" Rupert said out loud.

"What bell?" Folky asked.

"The big one. In the town square. Is it still there?"

"Yeah."

"Can you show me it?"

"Sure."

Folky strolled off, and Rupert followed. They jogged past the darkened road that curved just like it did back in his own time. They crossed a wide avenue lined with small shops and turned down well-lit streets that grew busier with each block.

At last, they came the town center. Rupert gasped out loud.

Wow. So, this is what Graysland used to be like.

A giant tree stood in the center of a circular street paved with blue cobblestones. The tree was taller than all the surrounding buildings and was aglow with colored lights and countless silver and gold trinkets. Ropes of lights were strung from poles to drape across the traffic circle to the corners of buildings.

At the base of the tree sat a bell bigger than Rupert had ever seen. It was as tall as he was and sparkled with reflections of all the lights. It was decorated with engravings of cat faces and moons similar to the ones on the little bell he had found in his yardback.

Dozens of townsfolk milled about, taking in the sights and enjoying the evening air. Rupert went for a closer view of the bell, and Folky, looking bored, followed. He could just make out his reflection in the polished chrome of its surface. A universe of Winter Joy lights sparkled in it.

"This is all so nice. Where I come from, it's all so boring. No one celebrates Winter Joy."

"So, you don't get gifts from Winter Cat?" Folky asked with a touch of pity.

"Nope. All we do is rake leaves."

"Hey, you wanna see what the Winter Cat brought me last year?"

"Okay."

"Follow me."

Folky raced off across the square and down a wide avenue lined with colorful Winter Joy lights of cherry, lemon and blueberry. The shops had window displays showing snowy landscapes with flying cats and starry skies.

Rupert tried to take it all in as he battled to keep up with Folky. He still couldn't believe this was his boring and dull town of Graysland. The colors and the very *unboring* sights and sounds were almost as amazing as Far-Myst.

Folky turned down a pretty lane lined with fancifully trimmed trees. They looked like giant lollipops, all the same size and shape, and they were still fresh and green.

At the end of the street, they went left, and Rupert recognized where he was. Just before him was old Crabstick's place, but it was freshly painted, and the grass and shrubbery were neatly trimmed. As Folky continued on, Rupert had a feeling in his gut where they were heading. Sure enough, they stopped at a huge mansion at the end of the street.

He was back on Old Homes Avenue, and he was standing before the old mansion where his adventure had begun. The one he had last seen belching flames from its upper window.

The house looked pretty much as when he'd seen it last. The overgrown trees and shrubs cascaded across the large plot of land where it sat. The only differences were that most of the oval windows glowed with lamplight, and the front door basked in the orange glow of two gas lamps that sat atop two carved stone gargoyles.

Folky ran to the front door and pushed it open, waving for Rupert to follow.

"So, *you're* the rich kid!" Rupert said with a bit of a chuckle.

"Just come in," Folky told him.

Rupert felt like he was reliving the scary moment when the man with the gun forced him and Squeem though this same doorway.

Inside, the main living room was brighter. There was no smell of wax and old cheese like he remembered. Instead, a delicious smell of cooking lingered in the air and teased his stomach.

A voice startled him.

"How many times do I have to warn you about storming in through the front door?"

"Oops, I forgot, Jethro!" Folky apologized.

Jethro was an older man, much older than Rupert's father. He was dressed in a long black jacket and a white shirt that made him look like a penguin.

"And who is this ragamuffin you have dragged in with you?"

"This is Rupert. Rupert, this is Jethro, our butler."

"Hi." Rupert offered meekly. He had no idea what a butler was but decided not to bother asking.

"I am not *your* butler, child. I am the butler for the master and his home."

"So, you live *here*?" Rupert asked Folky in a whisper.

"Sometimes," was the cryptic answer. "Come on, let me show you my room and what the Cat brought me!"

"Hold on just one moment!" Jethro said, stepping in front of them with a slight stumble of his old legs. "Your mother is worried sick about you. You make your presence known to her this instant!"

"Yes, Jethro," sang Folky.

"And offer your friend a glass of milk and a cookie. There's to be no rudeness under any roof I am responsible for!"

"Okay!"

Folky ran around the winding staircase, pulling Rupert along. He noticed that the paintings of the grumpy folks were not hanging on the walls. Instead, there were large paintings of castles and mysterious-looking towers.

They raced down a long hallway then a narrow, steep staircase as the smell of cooking grew stronger and even more delicious. Finally, after a maze of corridors, they entered a large kitchen.

A woman was mixing sauce in a clear glass bowl. Her sandy hair was tied in a bun, much like the way Rupert's mother wore hers but smaller and sort of like a snail shell the way it spiraled. She looked tired, but her pretty face was soft, and her eyes had a smile behind them.

She looked up, and her expression of relief was quickly replaced by a frown. She put the bowl down and came over to Folky.

"Where have you been? Do you know it's after ten?" She hugged Folky and gave Rupert a glance. She looked her daughter over head to foot. "What a dirty mess you are. One would think you were an orphan. And this ratty hat has to go!" She took the hat off Folky's head, and a long mop of sandy-blond hair cascaded down. "That's my girl. Why you insist on hiding your beautiful hair is beyond me."

"You're a girl!" Rupert said, trying to hide his amazement. He had noticed Folky's voice was sort of high but didn't think much of it, as some of his friends at school who were boys had high voices.

"No kidding?" Folky said with a knowing smirk. "Rupert, this is Sara, but I just call her Mom 'cause she is. Mom, this is Rupert. He says he's lost, but I think he's just a kook because he says he lives on that new street in a house that ain't even built yet—"

Rupert interrupted her. "I was just kidding."

Sara smiled. "Nice to meet you, Rupert. Have a fanciful imagination, huh? You two should get along quite well."

"Can I show Rupert my birds?" Folky asked.

"Get him a glass of milk and one of those brownies from lunch first. And just for ten minutes. I'm sure Rupert's parents are worried as well. And, Folka, wash those filthy hands of yours."

"It's Folky, Mom! I hate Folka. Sounds like somebody's grandmother's name."

Folka? Rupert thought.

"Folka *Tweenbort?*" he asked aloud.

"How do you know my last name?" Folky demanded.

Rupert stared, stunned. He studied the shape of her face. Her eyes *had* looked familiar.

His grandmother, the little sweet and wise old woman with the coffus and her patient ways, stood before him as a spirited eleven-year-old girl.

He wasn't sure if he wanted to scream or laugh out loud.

Chapter 11
Birds, Boos and Bells

Folky's room was smaller than Rupert's, but it was much cooler. At least, he thought so when he stepped into the narrow space lit by three oil lamps. There were no windows, as the room was below ground-level, but a slight breeze blew in from an ornate brass vent on the ceiling. Along one wall was a small cot-type bed and a small end table.

Across the room along the other wall were six cages, each holding a pair of colorful birds. The birds all grew excited and burst into chirping as Folky entered. They had feathers in all kinds of brilliant colors. Some were blue with yellow dabs while others were orange-and-black or red-and-green.

Rupert smiled and took a closer look.

"Wow, these are great. Never seen such colorful birds. At least not in this town." He decided it was best not to mention the amazing creatures he'd seen in Far-Myst.

"I let them fly around at night when everybody's a-sleep," Folky said, opening one of the cages and allowing a brilliant blue bird with drops of lemon-yellow on its wing-tips to jump onto her finger. She held it out to Rupert.

"This is Sheba. I stole her from that mean shop owner."

"Really?" Rupert smiled at how honest Folky could be.

"Yes. He never let her fly. She's the sweetest thing. She'll sing to me and even rub her head on mine. Go ahead, pet her."

Rupert put the last piece of brownie in his mouth and stroked the bird gently. She made a purring sound like a happy cat.

"So, how did you get so rich?" Rupert asked.

"I'm not. My mother is the cook for the rich man who owns this house. He lets us live here. My father was a fisherman…so he has to travel a lot. I don't get to see him that often." Folky's expression turned sad, but she covered it quickly with a smile.

"Your mom works late, huh?"

"It's Winter Joy time. Lots of food to make. She's making the fergooder gifts."

"The what?"

"The gifts you give to the nice neighbors. Or to poor people who have nothing. Mr. Starkey loves Winter Joy and buys lots of food for the people of Gracelandville."

Starkey? Could she mean Ensen Starkey? Rupert wondered.

"He's not a mean old man?" he asked.

"No. Why would you think that?"

Rupert shrugged and was about to change the subject when a strange howling sounded from the vent. It was like a sad cow mooing at the moon. Or perhaps the wind.

"What was that?" he asked.

"I think this house is haunted. I hear weird sounds sometimes."

"Well, that's definitely not boring," Rupert said.

Folky put Sheba back in the cage. There was a knock on the door. Sara peered in.

"Rupert. I think it's time for you to head home. Do you live far from here?"

He had no clue how to answer that question, so he just stared. Folky jumped in.

"I'll make sure he gets home, Mom."

Sara smiled and left. Rupert waited until all was clear then asked, "Can you show me where the ghost lives?"

"I hear him all over the house. But mostly in the secret staircase."

"Secret staircase?" Rupert asked with an excited smile.

"Wanna see it?"

"Yeah!"

Folky guided him down the hallway towards the kitchen but turned left and opened a door at the end of the hall. This led to a short, narrow passage that was lit only by the light pouring in from the open doorway. There was another door, and Folky pulled and yanked on it until it opened with a squeak of hinges. A spiral staircase awaited them that twisted up into darkness.

"These are the secret steps. Just hold on to the banister and be careful. Steps are steep." Folky explained.

Rupert nodded and followed her up into the stairwell. The air smelled like candles, and it reminded him of how the air smelled when he'd climbed the steps of the ruins of Elderwind Castle in Far-Myst.

It was dark, and he stepped carefully, using his foot to feel each step. He slid his hand along the smooth metal banister that was very cold to the touch.

"Where does this go?" he asked.

"To the widow's walk at the top."

"What's that?" Rupert wondered.

"It's the lookout place where people go to see the ships coming and going. They call it a widow's walk 'cause that's

55

where wives would go to see if their husbands were coming home from fishing or were dead. Drowned or eaten by a shark or something."

"Does your mother go up here to look for your dad?"

"Watch your step here, its broken."

There was a loud creak of wood as Folky stepped, and Rupert was extra-careful as he followed. He knew she had ignored his question about her father and decided not to ask her again.

The pitch-blackness started to fade as murky moonlight drifted down from above. Soon, Rupert's eyes adjusted, and he could see little paintings on the curving walls of the stairwell. They were all colorful, pretty scenes of forests and beaches and mountains.

Finally, Folky stepped into a square room surrounded on all four sides by windows. Light from the full round moon poured in through the glass. Rupert stepped beside her and was amazed by the lights of the town spread out below him.

"Wow, didn't know this house went up so high." he said.

"Look." Folky pointed. "If you look between those trees you can see some of the river. My mother says you used to be able to see the dock, but they built that building there and now you can't."

"Did you watch for your father coming home from fishing up here?"

Folky stared out the window a moment, silently, then shrugged.

"He died when I was three. His fishing boat sank."

"Oh," Rupert replied softly. "Sorry about that."

"I remember him a little. His face. His beard when he kissed my face. He smelled like fish and cinnamon all the time," she recalled with a smile.

"Why cinnamon?" Rupert asked.

"He loved my mother's cinnamon cookies. He would come here to the kitchen before every fishing trip, and my mom would give him a big bag of cookies. After he died, Mr. Starkey gave us rooms here so my mother could save up enough money to buy a house. Maybe we'll buy one on Curving Road like you." Folky rolled her eyes and gave Rupert a strange smirk.

"What?" he asked defensively.

"How can you live on Curving Road if none of the houses are finished?"

Rupert blushed and knew he either had to lie or tell the very complicated truth.

"I don't. I really live on Everstood Street," he lied, picking the first name that popped into his head.

"Never heard of it. Is it on the far end of town?"

"No. It's in a town called Graysland."

"Never heard of that, either. Did you run away from home?"

"Sort of," he said.

Suddenly, there was the sound of footsteps coming up from below. Rupert and Folky froze. They were slow, deliberate steps.

"Who's there?" Folky called out. "Is that you, Mr. Ensen?"

There was no response. The footsteps stopped, and all was dead silent for a moment. Then, a freezing breeze tussled the hair of both Rupert and Folky. They shivered and looked at each other.

"Maybe we should leave?" Rupert suggested.

"Yeah," Folky agreed, rushing off down the steps. Rupert raced after her.

They emerged from the staircase and looked at each other and giggled.

"That was kinda cool, " Rupert said. "Scary but not boring like my house!"

Folky nodded and headed down the hall. He followed.

As they moved towards the main part of the house, Rupert heard two men talking. The smell of something burning, much sweeter than logs in the fireplace, tickled his nose. They entered the living room and found the two men. One stood by the fireplace, and the other, his back to them, sat on a sofa.

"Hello, Folka," greeted the standing man. "You're up late."

"Just seeing my friend Rupert out. Hope you don't mind me using the front door?" Folky asked. She turned to Rupert. "Rupert, this is Mr. Ensen Starkey."

"Hello, Mr. Rupert."

The man held out his hand. Rupert took it. His grip was firm, and he shook Rupert's hand as if he were a man.

Ensen Starkey was about the same height as Rupert's father but leaner and more solidly built. His thinning silver hair was brushed back and slicked down. His face was handsome, and his eyes were dark, like coffee. He was dressed in a silk jacket and black slacks with crimson-red slippers. He held a pipe in his hand and let rings of sweet smoke waft from his lips as he spoke.

"Rupert, meet my friend, Mr. Bolton Gripper." Ensen gestured to the man on the sofa, who stood and faced them.

Rupert gasped. He hoped he hadn't done it too loudly, but he knew he had.

The man was dressed in a black, flowing cape. His face was bony, and his eyes ice-blue. He leaned closer, extending a thin hand, and smiled, revealing a mouth full of brown and broken teeth. One of his front teeth was capped with gold, and another had a large emerald fastened on it.

Rupert stared into his cold eyes and gingerly shook his hand. A shiver ran up his spine.

"Hello, Rupert. Very nice to meet you," Bolton Gripper said.

Rupert tried to reply but could only manage a nod. Gripper chuckled and went back to his sofa. There was a slight tinkle when he sat, a sound Rupert recognized.

Gripper removed the little bell from the sofa and placed it on the table before him.

Folky nudged Rupert and headed for the front door. They stopped on the steps.

"Go around the back and climb up to the third window on the second floor. You can sleep in there. Mr. Starkey never goes up there."

"What about Gripper?" Rupert asked, trying to control the frightened shiver in his voice.

"He doesn't live here. He just advises Mr. Starkey on his business. Go up, and I'll sneak you some more food. Okay?"

Rupert knew he had no choice, so he agreed. Folky went back inside and closed the door. He rushed to the rear of the house.

It was so weird. Just a few hours ago, he and Squeem had climbed down the drainpipe to escape the fire and the enraged Bolton Gripper. Now he was about to climb back up and spend the night in the house.

He took hold of the pipe and shimmied up to the ledge, which was cleaner and had much less weather damage than it had his last time around. The shutters were open on all the windows.

He tiptoed across to the third window; sure enough, it was the room he had been prisoner in. The window was already open, and he peeked in to see if the coast was clear. It was.

The room was set up as a small office. A solid redwood desk was in the center, and to one side were a comfy sofa and a fancy end table. A shelf was lined with thick black binders. The floor was covered with carpeting with a pattern like a fall of autumn leaves.

Rupert rushed to the door, turned the knob quietly and opened the door a crack. The hallway outside was silent. He closed it and found a chair and braced it under the knob.

The room was lit with an oil lamp that hung above the desk. He discovered that if he turned a small knob the wick would be extended and the flame would brighten. He scanned the binders on the shelf.

Each had a strip of white tape on the spine with a handwritten label. They said things like First Quarter *Sales. Inventory. Manifest. Loans.* Words he had heard his father use when discussing his coffin business and all too boring for Rupert.

But one binder had a name that struck his fancy. It was titled *Winter Joyous.* He took it off the shelf and opened it. It was a handwritten manuscript.

His eyes almost fell out of his head as he read the name of the author, printed neatly below the title.

Mookie Starbright.

Rupert smiled, and he took the manuscript with him to the comfy sofa. He sat down and began to read.

Chapter 12
Winter Joyous

Winter Joyous
by Mookie Starbright

There are few times of the year that fill me with as much vim and happiness as does the day when the Winter Cat roams our star-filled skies. I would be saddened to meet the poor chap who has never enjoyed the aroma of steaming-hot coberberry-glazed turnip pasties or tasted savory steamed garlic-mustard scallops wrapped in sweet bacon.

Sadder still would I be for the soul who had never seen the face of a poverty-stricken child smiling at the fergooder gifts handed to his appreciative parents.

Then, of course, who cannot be awed by the magic of the trinket tree, glistening under moonlight awaiting the gifts

61

of Aranthal the Winter Cat. Or the smiles and kindness of strangers that abound in the busy squares of our city.

Nay, I have not yet met this unfortunate person but would take their hand and guide them through the season myself so as to not let them die without having their hearts sing with Winter Joy.

A strange squeal yanked Rupert from his reading. It sounded like a cat calling out in the night and was coming from one of the other rooms. He sat frozen as it grew louder and louder; it was coming from the other side of the wall across from the desk.

He got up and listened, cocking his head. The squealing stopped. A panel in the wall lifted open, and he thought his heart was going to shoot out of his nostrils!

Sitting on a platform was a plate of food—a fried chicken leg, a hunk of cheese, crackers and a tall glass of lemonade. Rupert smiled and grabbed the plate as Folky's whisper echoed up the dumbwaiter shaft so clearly it was as if she were in the room.

"Goodnight, Rupert!"

"Thanks, Folky!" Rupert whispered back.

The little platform lowered, and the panel closed.

He spent the next hour enjoying his meal and reading more of Mookie Starbright's thoughts on The Winter Joy. He learned the holiday had been celebrated in Gracelandville for many, many years . Almost all the people would decorate a tree near their homes with trinkets and await the arrival of Aranthal, the cat created by Mother Joy—a special woman who lived in a mystical place called Venjurus that was far, far away in an unknown land.

She had fashioned Aranthal from a lump of snow to help her spread joy and happiness by leaving small gifts for everyone who had done acts of charity or showed kindness to their neighbors. People would light special candles and share food with neighbors. They rang the gildens until two stars called the Eyes of Aranthal shone brightly overhead in the sky. Then the giant bell would be rung in the town square, and all the folks would head to bed to await the visit by Aranthal.

Rupert fell in love with Winter Joy. He could not imagine a reason why people would stop celebrating such a wonderful thing.

His mind drifted; the words on the page went out of focus, and his thoughts of Winter Joy mixed and blended with thoughts of Mookie. Why was Mookie's book here? Did he live nearby? He thought about the cat, and how cool it would be to have gifts brought to his house on The Curving Road and placed under his banberry tree, decorated with all kinds of trinkets.

He felt a rush of excitement—a bubbling in his stomach and electricity flowing in his body. He could see the magical cat Aranthal flying out of the sky with a big smile and, like a comet, swoop down his street.

He opened his eyes. Sitting on the desk was a small glass globe that had not been there just moments ago. Rupert slowly approached it and took it in his hands. Inside was a small cat made of some silver metal. It was sitting the way cats do, and it stared out at Rupert, a toothy kitty smile on its face. Rupert gazed back and wondered if it had just appeared or if it had been sitting there the entire time.

No, he decided. It had not been there. It just appeared. *Did my Imaginings create it? But I wasn't really trying.*

Yet there it was.

The sound of two men talking snatched his attention from the glass ball. He followed the voices to a metal vent low in the wall behind the desk. He recognized Ensen and

Gripper. Their voices were clear, and they seemed to be involved in a discussion that was getting more and more heated.

"I have been telling you this for years," Gripper said in his raspy voice. "You must remove the heart of the season. You are in position to take control of Winter Joy!"

"That will be going too far, Gripper. The bell is an important symbol for the folks of Gracelandville." Ensen replied.

"Yes, It is. And it should be removed from the eyes of the people and brought here."

"How would I accomplish that?"

"You are the richest man in town. How do you think?" Gripper's voice was becoming more of a growl.

"I am quite content with things as they are, Gripper."

"Content? Never. Do not forget that you are in my debt."

"And don't *you* forget, Gripper — you owe me as well."

"Yesss," Gripper hissed. He went silent suddenly.

"What's wrong?" Ensen asked.

Without warning, the snow globe grew very warm. Rupert discovered the eyes of the cat were glowing bright red. He heard footsteps climbing the staircase then moving toward the door of his room. He sat frozen as whoever it was stopped outside his door.

Rupert didn't breathe. He stared at the door and hoped the chair would be enough to hold back Gripper should he decide to enter. The cat's eyes glowed brighter, and Rupert remembered the fortune seeds from Far-Myst and how they would glow red if dark Imaginings were near. He wondered if the cat worked the same way.

He could now hear Grippers raspy breathing; he was mumbling something under his breath. A gray mist came creeping under the door. It was like smoke but more ghost-like. Rupert watched in horror as the mist formed into two bony arms with claw-like hands!

Then a head materialized, and its face was terrible to look at. Misty eyes stared at Rupert, and the ghostly specter smiled devilishly. Rupert wanted to look away or close his eyes, but he couldn't.

He held tight to the glass globe and imagined that the face wasn't there. He imagined a strong wind blowing in through the window and shoving the ghost back under the door where it came from.

"Go away. Go away," Rupert whispered.

The face moved closer, and the smile was changing into a frown.

"*Go away!*" Rupert said forcibly under his breath.

The sound of wind filled his ears, and in a flash, the smoky demon collapsed into a shapeless cloud and poured back under the door. There was a grunt, an evil chuckle, and then footsteps that faded to silence. Rupert allowed himself to breath and tiptoed to the vent and listened.

"Why did you go upstairs?" Ensen asked.

"I thought I heard the little feet of a scurrying rat. Seems I was wrong. I am leaving. We will discuss our business tomorrow."

Rupert heard the front door open and close.

He sat back on the sofa and tried to get comfortable; he would be sleeping on it all night. He looked at the cat in the globe, and its eyes went back to normal, their glow fading.

He wondered if this room made his Imaginings possible. It was here, after all, that he'd seen Pie O'Sky's face in the window.

He set his thoughts back to that colorful, mysterious man. Why did he provide the door for Rupert to go back to the past of Graysland? Did Pie O'Sky want Winter Joy to return? Why?

He had assumed Pie O'Sky was from Far-Myst and was only concerned with their problems. But maybe Pie O'Sky cared about everybody's problems. Maybe he had grown fond of Rupert and heard his wish and came to help?

Rupert reached for the key that had appeared on the chain around his neck, and it was gone.

So many thoughts and questions swam around in his brain. Who was Gripper? What did he really want? Could Mookie Starbright have an answer? Could Rupert find Mookie?

So many thoughts were making his head hurt. He needed to sleep. He set his mind on Imagining the morning. The sun would be warm, and the birds would sing. He would try to get some answers then.

Chapter 13

Red, Sparkling Tines

As Rupert had imagined, morning came with warm sunlight and tweeting birds. The brilliant beams of sun nudged him awake. It took him a few seconds to realize where he was. He got up, stretched, yawned, and went to the door and listened. All was quiet.

There was a fancy little clock on the desk made of polished silver metal that read ten minutes past seven. The sound of the dumbwaiter rising behind the wall caught his attention, and when the panel opened, he smiled at the sight of a plate of scrambled eggs, bacon and toast. There was a tall glass of orange juice as well. A handwritten note sat folded beside the glass.

> *After you eat breakfast meet me near the red shed behind the house. Mr. Starkey has already left, and Jethro has the eyes of a bat but the*

ears of a cat so be quiet! The maid will be up to clean soon so put all dirty dishes back on dumb waiter.

Folky

P.S. You can use the bathroom at the end of the hall.

Rupert was happy to hear there was a bathroom near. He removed the chair from the door and quietly opened it a crack.

The hallway was empty, so he tiptoed down to the bathroom and took care of business. He needed a few moments to figure out how to flush the old toilet until he discovered the pull chain hanging up near the ceiling where a water tank was. He washed his face and rinsed his mouth then quietly made his way back to the room, where he devoured his delicious breakfast.

He put the dishes and glasses from last night's snack on the tray with the breakfast dishes and slid it onto the dumbwaiter and closed the panel. He put on his jacket, tucked the glass ball with the cat into his pocket and went to the window. It easily lifted open. A wonderful blast of fresh air washed across his face. It was chilly, but it felt good. He stepped out onto the ledge.

In daylight, the property seemed much smaller than it had in the dark. However, the gardens, overgrown with shrubs and vines, stretched out more than three times the area of his own yardback at home.

Home.

It was such a strange thing, Rupert thought. Here he was, less than a mile from 17 The Curving Road, and yet he was so much farther away from it on the calendar. Eighty years!

He quickly spotted the tool shed, painted a bright cherry red, and strolled to it. The door was fastened with a padlock, so he just stood beside it, his hands in his pockets, and waited.

He gripped the glass ball. It felt cold, and Rupert assumed that was a good thing. No dark Imaginings around. He shivered as he thought about the ghostly smoke that had slipped into the room last night. He wondered who Gripper was and what kind of nasty powers he might have.

The sound of rustling leaves interrupted his thoughts. He saw Folky approaching, dressed in a green coat, brown pants and her old hat. Her hair hung loose, and she looked like a girl as her soft face shone in the bright sun.

That's my grandmother, how crazy is that? Rupert thought, laughing in his mind.

"What's so funny?" Folky asked stepping up to the shed opening it with a key.

Rupert blushed—he hadn't realized the laughter in his mind had lifted a smile on his face.

"Nothing, just thinking about something."

Folky shrugged and removed two rakes from the shed. They were things of beauty his father would have drooled over! They had sparkling red tines, and their pinewood handles were polished and bright. The handles were capped with shimmering brass, with a loop to hang them on hooks. Painted on the wooden handle were the words *E.S. Inc. Farm Tools.*

"Are you going back home today?" Folky asked.

"Not sure. I am sorta lost."

"Lost? I thought you said you lived on Curving Road?"

"Well, yes, but…"

"But what?"

"You saw. The houses aren't built yet. I'm *gonna* live there. One day."

Folky was trying to understand.

69

"So, where do you live *this* day?"

Rupert wasn't sure what to tell her.

"Here," he said, gesturing at the house. "So, what time do you have to go to school?"

"I don't. It's Saturday. Take this."

She handed him one of the rakes, and he reacted as if she'd handed him a live squid.

"What am I supposed to do with this?"

"What do you think" Folky asked, pushing the rake into Rupert's hand. "Pick your nose?"

"I didn't think people raked leaves back now."

"Back now? What's that suppose to mean?"

"I mean...here. This town," Rupert said as he took hold of the rake and tried to control his blush.

"Well, we never really thought much about it. But when Mr. Starkey's factory started to lose money because not so many people have farms anymore, he figured he should start making rakes, since so many people just let leaves pile up. See?" She pointed at the words on the handle. "E.S., Inc. That's Ensen Starkey."

She led Rupert to the front lawn, where she began to rake the leaves that were scattered across the browning grass. Rupert stood watching.

"Just 'cause he makes the rakes don't mean people are gonna feel like raking."

"That's what Mr. Starkey said. So Mr. Gripper told him he has to make them make a law that we all have to rake our leaves every day. Then everybody would have to buy one, and he would make lots more money."

"How is he gonna do that?" Rupert asked.

Folky shrugged and continued raking until she noticed he was just watching. She kicked a bunch of leaves at his feet, and he rolled his eyes.

"Just like home," he moaned as he began his chore.

"So, did you sleep okay?"

"Yeah. Sort of. That thing kind of freaked—" Rupert stopped himself. He wanted to tell her about the ghostly form but wasn't sure he should.

"What?" Folky asked with a growing smile. "Did you see the ghost?"

He nodded.

"What did it look like?" she asked with great excitement.

"It was smoky. Came under the door." Rupert lowered his voice. "That scary Gripper guy was right outside when it happened."

"Really? Never saw one like that."

"That Gripper guy gives me the creeps. Is he around here all the time?"

"No. Just when he has to talk to Mr. Starkey about business. He has an office in the town center. Near the bell."

"Can I ask you something?"

Folky stopped raking.

"Do your auntie and uncle live close by? The ones who have the Mookie Starbright books?"

She looked at him as if he had kittens crawling out of his nose.

"Who?"

Rupert's heart skipped a beat. His grandmother had told him she'd seen Mookie's *Just Because* books when she'd visited her aunt and uncle's house. But when? She might not have done that yet!

"Ummm…" He tried to act natural. "I found this book in the room upstairs. Written by a guy named Mookie Starbright."

"I never heard of him. How do you know my auntie and uncle live nearby?"

"I guess I just have a good imagination. Made it up."

"You're a kook-a-doo, Rupert. Come on, let's get this raking done. What should we do today? I can show you the stream where the green frogs live!"

71

"Can we go back to the big bell?"

"Again?"

"I love all the Winter Joy decorations. We don't have that stuff where I come from."

"Okay, I guess," Folky said with little excitement. Then her eyes brightened as she got an idea. "You can help me give out some of the fergooder gifts! My mother made all kinds of yummy stuff. With two of us, it will take half the time, and then we can go find frogs!"

"Cool." Rupert was glad. He liked frogs, although no frog in Graysland (or Gracelandville) could ever top the hummdrummers he'd seen in Far-Myst. The only regular frog he ever saw was in Mr. Bunsenburn's science class, and it was stuffed and sat in a jar of greenish liquid.

He was more excited he'd be able to get back to the town center where all the people were. People who might be able to help him find Mookie Starbright.

He smiled, took hold of the rake and let its shiny red tines begin gathering the many colorful leaves that carpeted the lawn.

Chapter 14

Into the Shadows

The town center had a very different feel in daylight. All the Winter Joy lights that shone with brilliant colors in the dark of night now hung like unripened fruit. It was all still pretty, but there was none of the magical sparkle.

There were, however, many more people about. All the stores and little open-air shops were busy; and kids, dogs, and a cat or two sniffed around for treats. A flock of pigeons scattered as a rambunctious little boy disturbed their meal of bread crumbs tossed by an old couple sitting on a pair of milk crates. Many wonderful aromas drifted around Graystone Circle.

The bell sat as it had the previous night, but now its sheen reflected the clear blue of the sky.

Rupert and Folky were both carrying large packages of treats. Rupert drooled as the scents of cinnamon and maple tickled his nose.

"I'll show you how to do it, then we can split up and get all the fergooder gifts handed out. Okay?"

"Okay." He nodded.

Folky guided him across the circle to Needswork Street, a narrow road lined with four-story brick buildings. Many were in need of fresh paint or new glass to replace cracked or broken windows.

"This used to be called Pleasant Tree Lane. Not sure why they changed the name. Pretty boring, if you ask me," Folky said as she stopped before building number 39. She knocked on the front door. Soon a little boy around eight appeared, dressed in old shorts and a baggy shirt.

"Who are you?" he asked with a distrusting glare.

"Is your mommy or daddy home?" Folky asked with a big smile.

"Yeah. Ma! There's some dumb kids at the door!" the boy shouted.

A pale woman appeared and smiled when she spotted Folky.

"Hello, Folga. Have an ashishtant thish year, huh?" she said. Spit appeared on her lips, which she wiped with her sleeve.

Folky took a package from the large bundle. It was wrapped in pretty blue paper decorated with silver stars.

"This is for you. Joyous Winter to you and your family. May the Cat treat you well."

"Thank you, shweetie. And pleashe wish your mother a Happy Winter Joy for me. She ish a shpecial lady."

"I will. Oh, this is my friend Rupert Dullz."

"Hello," Rupert said shyly.

"Hello, Mr. Dullz. Are you related to Barnaby Dullz?"

"Not that I know of," Rupert said.

"Good," the woman smiled. "He'sh a pain in the rump roasht."

Rupert smiled, and Folky chuckled.

"Well, see you around, Mrs. Beezle," Folky said.

The woman thanked them again and closed the door.

Mrs. Beezle? Rupert wondered if she was a relative of Squeem.

Folky turned to him.

"Are you ready to split up and deliver on your own?"

"I guess so."

"Good. The addresses are written on the packages. Number sixty-five is that way." She pointed. "I'll meet you at the bell in an hour."

Rupert had just started off when Folky shouted, "And remember — smile!"

He turned and nodded then headed down Needswork Street.

Number 65 was a shorter building, only two stories, and looked like it might be the oldest one on the street. Its wooden siding looked sad with its chipping and peeling yellow paint that at one time must have been very happy.

He knocked on the door, and soon a bald man with lots of stubbly whiskers down his neck appeared. He rubbed his big belly and belched before he said hello.

"Hello, Mister. My name is Rupert Dullz, and I wish to wish you a very joyous Winter Joy." Rupert knew he sounded like he was reading from a blurry blackboard and tried to breathe and relax.

The man didn't reply or even change his expression.

"I want to give you this fergooder gift from my grandma's — I mean, from Folky's mother as a gift to you and your family."

Rupert held out the package, and the man eventually took it from him. He managed a tiny smile.

"You know, I been outta work for a while. Normally, I give out fergooder gifts myself."

Rupert could sense the man was embarrassed.

"My mom was out of work once, and she felt bad. But she got another job. A better one! And I bet you will, too."

75

The man studied Rupert a moment before he smiled warmly. He belched and nodded a *thank you*. As he was about to return inside, Rupert called him back to answer a question.

"Mister, do you know a man named Mookie Starbright?"

The man pondered the name a few seconds then shook his head. Rupert started to leave.

"Hey, kid!" the man said. Rupert turned to see him give a thumb's-up. He smiled and headed off.

His next stop was 55 Shadow Lane, a narrow passage that cut Needswork Street in half. It lived up to its name. The street got very little sunlight, and dark splotches of shadow hung around like nasty things waiting to pounce. Litter lay scattered like autumn leaves. The doorways were sunk in cubbyholes that had steps leading down to them.

He searched for number 55, but none of the buildings had numbers, or when they did they were faded so much they were impossible to read.

He heard a door lock unlatch and spotted a man emerging from a ten-story building whose front was caked with ancient grime. The man, dressed in a black trench coat, was bald and wore a patch over one eye and had a large scar across his cheek. He eyed Rupert and walked off.

"Excuse me!" Rupert called out.

The man turned and glared at him suspiciously. He held something in his hand that glinted gold. He quickly shoved it under his coat but said nothing.

"I'm looking for number fifty-five."

"I don't know nothing about it," the man said as he slithered off.

Rupert made a face at him. A sudden flare of warmth from his pocket nudged his attention. He slipped his hand in and felt the glass ball heating up. He smiled wide.

Ever since returning from Far-Myst, he'd felt a need for adventure. True, he was scared, but he needed to peek inside the building. The hotter the glass ball with the cat grew, the more he couldn't resist exploring.

He quietly walked down the three steps, took hold of the doorknob and opened the door. As he entered, he didn't see Gripper watching him with shifty eyes from a window on the second floor.

The moment he stepped inside, Rupert was smacked across the face with the smell of something burning. It wasn't leaves or charcoal or a slab of chewybeef, like when his father burned it on the BBQ. It was pungent, sharp. Like a knife. Like metal.

Voices, numerous and of various tones, bounced down the long hallway that faced him. The corridor was barely lit by three reddish electric light bulbs that hung from the ceiling by old, dirty wires. Doors lined both walls. A pulsing noise, like some sort of machine, came from the open door at the far end.

He hurried as quietly as he could, the package of fergooder gifts under one arm and his hand checking the globe in his pocket. It was growing hotter. As he moved closer to the mechanical beat another pulse got faster and louder — his own heart, pounding like a drum.

The smell of burning metal was stronger.

When Rupert made it to the door, he peered in, and his eyes widened. The room was long and divided into three areas by chain-link fences. The first section contained a large vat of bubbling silver metal. Men dressed in black garments were carefully and slowly pouring the hot metal into molds.

In the middle section, workers removed objects from a moving conveyor belt. Bells. Silver bells. In the final section, people screwed on the little wooden handles while others placed completed bells into individual boxes.

Rupert jumped when a hand fell on his shoulder. He spun around to find a short, stocky man—much shorter than he was, glaring up at him.

"Who are you, child?"

"Uh, I was just looking for building number fifty-five."

"Well, this isn't it. You come with me."

The little man grabbed Rupert firmly by the arm and tried to drag him down an intersecting hallway. Rupert gave a wicked kick to the man's shin. He yelped in pain and let go. Rupert raced off toward the door…and slammed into a black wall.

He looked up and discovered the wall was staring down at him with a broken-toothed smile—a smile with an emerald flashing on one front tooth.

Gripper took Rupert by the shoulders.

"Relax, my good lad. Why are you running like a pack of rabid dogs is on your tail?"

"I'm late. I need to deliver these gifts," Rupert said, trying to control his breathing.

The little man jogged up huffing and puffing.

"This runt was spying on us!"

"I wasn't! I swear! I am trying to find building fifty-five."

"That's fine, son." Gripper frowned at the little man. "Off with you! Back to work!"

The little man nodded nervously and rushed off. Rupert tried to take advantage of the moment and slip around Gripper but was stopped by a firm but gentle grasp on his arm that swept him back.

Gripper smiled again.

"Ah, delivering fergooder gifts! Good lad. Acts of charity are so…" He searched for the right word for a moment. "...charming. Did you see my workers making the bells?"

Rupert wasn't sure if he should answer.

"It's not a secret. The gildens are made here so all the good folks can ring them as the Winter Joy draws near. These are very special bells. They will not be not complete until they are coated with a thin layer of gold. Special gold. Mr. Starkey's company brings it in from the mines near Geeldings Bay.

"We are waiting for the next delivery of this magical gold to finish them. Only one bell has been coated with a small sample of the gold so far. "

"I thought Mr. Starkey made rakes and farm stuff," Rupert said.

"Well, the farm stuff is not as lucrative as it once was, so Mr. Starkey had to diversify his business. Do you know what *diversify* means?"

"Means different stuff, right?"

"Smart boy. Yes. And rakes are going to become a popular item very soon. Will become popular Winter Joy gifts. I bet you would like a shiny new rake from the Cat."

Rupert shook his head and forced a smile.

"I'm not from around here. Where I come from, we don't celebrate Winter Joy. But I wish we did, because it sounds cool."

Gripper studied him curiously then asked, "Where *are* you from?"

Rupert tried to stop himself but the word slipped out too fast.

"Graysland."

Gripper's eyebrows raised then his forehead wrinkled.

"Interesting. Graysland. Name is very familiar. Are you friends with Mr. Starkey? I am sure we have met before."

"I'm friends with Folky. We met last night at Mr. Starkey's house."

"Ah, yes, of course! My memory is not what it once was," Gripper said, smiling. "Folka. Fine young girl. She has a bright imagination. How about you, child? I suspect *you* have a wondrous imagination."

Rupert shrugged.

"Yes. I suspect you do. Well, I am sure you have more errands to run."

"I do."

Gripper stepped aside, and Rupert rushed for the door.

"Son? What is your name?" Gripper called after him.

Rupert paused with his hand on the doorknob.

"Rupert."

"Well, Rupert, I hope you have a very happy Winter Joy. Many changes are coming. Changes that will make Graysland—excuse me, Gracelandville—a much better place."

Rupert nodded and exited as fast as he could.

Chapter 15

The Hammer Head

Rupert wanted nothing but to get off creepy Shadow Lane.
He felt the sunlight hug him like an old friend as he went
back onto Needswork Street. He still had time to deliver
the five remaining fergooder gifts and meet Folky by the
bell.

His mind was racing. What sort of magical gold was
Gripper referring to? What about the object the bald man
with the eye patch had been holding? It was gold. Was it
one the special bells Gripper mentioned? What had Gripper meant when he said many changes were coming?

As if thinking about him had made him real, Rupert
spotted the bald man with the eye patch walking down the
opposite side of the street. Rupert could tell he was still
hiding something under his long flowing coat.

A tall, stocky man standing outside the Hook In Water Fish Shop bellowed, "Hey, Wurmzy!"

The bald man turned, and the fish seller, who wore a
blood-covered apron and a sweat- and bloodstained T-

shirt, waved him over. Rupert slipped into a nearby doorway and watched.

"Do you have it?" the fish seller asked, his voice low.

"You're gonna get me in some serious trouble, Brooch,"
Wurmzy said, scanning the street nervously.

"Shoulda thought o' that before you borrowed all that
cash. Either gimme the thousand or what you're hiding
under your coat." Brooch tapped the large knife that hung
from his belt.

Wurmzy looked up and down the street again then
took out what he held under his coat and handed it to
Brooch.

"Not my problem what happens," he warned as he
raced off down the street. Brooch smiled and returned to
his shop. Rupert followed him.

Rupert felt he was back home as the smell of fresh
fish swept up his nostrils. His parents often shopped here,
although the name had been changed to The Fish Store.
Mr. Able Scalesman owned it in Rupert's time; and perhaps Brooch was his father or even his grandfather. They
were the same size and shape.

One wall was lined with large metal trays loaded with
all sorts of colorful fish lying on thick beds of crushed ice.
The counter was covered with paper, and shelves were
stacked with jars and cans of various foods that folks might
eat with a fish meal.

But one thing was very different, something that didn't
exist in Rupert's memory of the store. Covering one wall
was a colorful and exciting mural of an undersea land-
scape—sharks, barracudas, sawfish, hammerheads, and
swordfish. Redfish, bluefish, purplefish, yellowfish and
a giant octopus were displayed in all their glory.

The colors were so bright and alive the painting would
have been at home on the walls of Everstood Castle in Far-
Myst. He stared at it in awe and wondered why it would

be painted over with dull, off-white paint years in the future.

"Pretty nifty painting, huh, kid?" Brooch said.

Rupert turned.

"Yeah. Who painted it?"

"Some guy named Starbright."

Rupert suddenly felt like one of the red snappers on the ice with their big mouths hanging open.

"Do you know where he lives?"

"Nope. Never met him. Painted that before I bought this place. Name's written right there on the bottom."

Rupert scanned the painting, and sure enough, in tiny, simple print in one lower corner were the two words that had sparked his Imagination — *Mookie Starbright*.

He then spotted the object, lying on a table behind the counter, peeking out of its black cloth wrapper. He knew what it was.

Brooch suddenly got antsy.

"So, you here to buy fish or look at artwork? This is a shop, not a museum."

Rupert hadn't had a chance to think of an excuse, so he mumbled and stumbled for a bit. Finally, his glance fell on the address written on one of the fergooder gifts.

"Do you know where thirty-four Closing Street is?"

"Yeah, two blocks left then make a right."

The front door bells rang as a young man with a mop of black hair and a clipboard entered.

"Morning, Brooch," he said. "Got today's catch. Some gorgeous bluebacks."

Brooch nodded and looked at Rupert.

"Okay, kid, I got work to do. Scram it."

Rupert nodded and exited the store. As he did, he overheard the hushed conversation between Brooch and the delivery man.

"Gotta unload quick, get back dockside. Hammer's taking a run to Geelding's Bay for another load."

Rupert's mind raced. Geelding's Bay! That was where the gold for the bells came from.

The fish delivery wagon waited at the curb outside the shop. The two large horses that pulled it, one black and one white, were drinking from a trough next to the sidewalk. Across the side of the wagon were the words *Monger Moe's Fish* in bright yellow letters. An address was beneath it: 444 South Riverside Road. Rupert knew about South Riverside. The name was the same in his day.

It was way too far to walk there and get back in time to meet Folky. He wondered if he should deliver the rest of the fergooder gifts and ask her to join him? Could he even tell her about the strange bells, and creepy Gripper, and Mookie Starbright?

He strolled casually around to the back of the wagon and tested the door. It was unlocked!

Rupert heard the door bells of Brooch's shop jingle and watched the fish delivery man exit the shop and climb up onto the cart. With a crack of the reins, the cart rolled off.

Rupert jogged behind the slow-moving wagon and grabbed the door handle in the back. The door swung open, and a blast of cold, fishy air blew into his face. There was a small step, and he tried to balance one foot on it and pull himself up.

The horses were picking up speed. He had to go for it and fast. He desperately tried to keep hold of the fergooder gifts under one arm while hanging on with all his might. A pothole was *not* what he needed.

The bundle of gifts flew from his grip and tumbled and scattered all over the cobblestone street behind him. Rupert, though, had more pressing concerns — like keeping his body from doing the same thing!

He grabbed hold of the other door handle and yanked himself up. The horses were by now almost in full gallop, and it was a struggle to finally get both feet inside on the wagon's ice-covered floor. He plopped down on his butt and looked out the back, frowning at the sight of the tasty treats lying like road kill.

The interior of the wagon was lined with freezing-cold metal, and just a couple of crates of fish, covered in ice, remained. The smell, however, surrounded him.

Am I crazy? Rupert wondered. *Folky is gonna be so mad at me, and her mother will never let me in the house again.*

The wagon turned off the cobblestone street and onto a slightly smoother dirt road. They rode beneath overhanging trees, some of the branches scraping the sides of the wagon. Finally, after twenty minutes or so, the river came into view, and they were rolling along South Riverside Road.

Rupert watched in awe as sailing ships cruised by. Tugboats and steamers he had only seen in schoolbooks were right before his eyes! That bubbling feeling of adventure was tickling his stomach.

His mind flashed to Pie O'Sky and riding in his colorful bagoon, and he wondered where that mysterious man was. Out of habit, he scanned the sky and saw nothing but a few seagulls circling overhead.

The fishwagon turned onto a narrow side street and stopped underneath a wooden overhang. Rupert's heart pounded. Should he make a run for it? He decided to quietly close the doors.

He heard the driver dismount and come around to the back. The footsteps stopped, and the door handle moved. Rupert flattened himself against the cold wall panel and held his breath.

The right-side door opened.

"Ah, this can wait," the man said. He closed the door.

Rupert exhaled with relief as the man's steps faded away. He opened the door a crack. The wagon was parked under a shelter beside a small shack. Beyond that, a boat bobbed in the water. He jumped out.

A bunch of men were unloading boxes from the boat. It was named the *Hammerhead*; the name was painted in red on its port side near the stern. It was not a giant ship nor was it a tiny skip. It was a medium-sized fishing boat that could easily house a dozen people. There were no sails, only a bright-red smoke stack rising high above its deck.

A stocky man in a black coat, a beanie clamped atop his round head, strolled up to the *Hammerhead,* put his hands on his hips and eyed the men.

"Are you idiots done yet? We have water to break and parcels to load!" he bellowed. "Have to be back before sunset, you water rats! I want to share my dinner with my family, not you smelly rascatillians!"

"Aye, Captain Stormwatch!" the men replied as they began working faster.

Before sunset. That's not so bad, Rupert thought. If he could get aboard and stay hidden, he might get some clues about the magical gold and the mysterious bells Gripper was making.

Captain Stormwatch stepped aboard his boat. Most of the crew had followed the captain. Rupert had to make his move if he was going with them on their trip to Geelding's Bay.

Two wooden planks led onto the deck of the boat, one at the bow and one at the stern. Rupert decided to make a run onto the rear one then hide in a group of large barrels that sat out on deck. Like a cat, he raced across the wooden pier and up the plank.

He was really scared for a moment when he discovered he couldn't lift the lids on any of the barrels. Finally, though, one gave way, and he was happy to discover the barrel was empty. He climbed inside.

The barrels were almost as tall as he was, so he fit inside easily and quite comfortably. His nose wrinkled at the seaweed smell. Through the opening of the barrel, he could see a swatch of sky and the tip-top of the smokestack. He could hear the chitter and chatter of the busy crew readying for departure.

There was a blast of thick steam from the smokestack. Ropes were pulled and coiled, and footsteps abounded. Soon, Rupert felt a soft, watery bounce as the *Hammerhead* moved out onto the river.

A cat meowed. Rupert looked up just in time to see an orange-and-white kitty jump onto the rim of the barrel then plop down into his lap. He began nuzzling Rupert's neck with a loud motorboat-like purr.

"Hey, buddy. You have to quiet down that purring of yours," Rupert whispered.

The cat couldn't have cared less. He continued giving Rupert wet sloppy kisses across his face. Rupert controlled his giggling. A metallic tinkle sounded, and he spotted a name tag hanging from the cat's collar. It read *McCoy*.

"Okay, McCoy, we have to stay quiet until we get to Geelding's Bay."

McCoy purred some more then curled into a ball on Rupert's lap.

Chapter 16

Terrible Gold

The *Hammerhead* cruised along for two hours before Rupert felt the boat slowing down. All he had seen during the journey was blue sky and a few puffy clouds overhead that slowly grew darker and blacker. A slow rain began to fall, and McCoy decided he'd had enough and took off for a dryer corner to nap in.

Rupert peeked over the rim of the barrel and scanned the deck. It was quiet, although he could hear voices coming from below. He looked out over the railing of the boat and couldn't believe his eyes. The boat was passing through a narrow channel past thick, dense trees and foggy land. The trees were ancient-looking, and many of the branches, like creepy hands, reached out towards the *Hammerhead*.

Where are we? Rupert wondered. He had never heard of Geelding's Bay, and he had certainly never heard about a creepy place like this anywhere near Graysland.

The space between the shore and the ship grew smaller and smaller, and soon Rupert could hear animal sounds coming from deep in the dense forest. Finally, the waterway widened, and they came upon an ancient stone building. It was built into the side of a hill and overgrown with thick brush. A decrepit pier, held together by algae and dead vines, awaited the Hammerhead.

Rupert had to think quickly. Soon the deck would be busy, and his chances of getting caught would be high. As the ship slowly brushed the side of the pier with a dull screech, he closed his eyes to think of a plan. He had to Imagine something.

He reached into his jacket and took out the glass ball. It was hot, and the cat's eyes were ruby-red. Something dark and scary lay ashore.

Only the sound of the rain disrupted the eerie quiet that blanketed the land around him. There were no crewmen rushing around on deck. Not yet. He needed to explore the boat and get some answers. He needed to move around quietly, invisibly.

He shook the sphere, and a wash of snow swirled around the little cat. The cat—even its red eyes—vanished behind the wall of white flakes. Rupert thought how cool it would be if he could Imagine snow that would swirl around him and make him invisible. Only, the snow would also be invisible, so he could wander around as he pleased and not be seen.

Rupert focused his mind, and a wall of invisible snow, swirling like a cyclone, moved across the world, blanking out everything it passed. It surrounded him, and in his mind, he became as clear as water. A soft whirring sound filled his ears, and he opened his eyes. Looking up at the sky, he saw a slight flickering. He looked down at himself.

He was gone! His arms, his legs, his entire body were invisible. He could feel a slight tingle swirling all around him. His Imaginings had done it again!

89

Rupert climbed out of the barrel and walked briskly across the wet deck, his invisible feet splashing in the occasional little puddles. Stairs led below the deck, and he quietly descended.

The steps led to a narrow passage with two doors on each side. At the end was an open area where hushed voices were busy in a discussion. The ceiling was quite low, and Rupert could easily reach out and touch it.

He made his way toward the voices, checking all the time to make sure he was still invisible. He was. When he reached the end of the passage, he was looking into the galley of the boat, where the captain and the crew sat around a large table. McCoy was curled up in a ball on Captain Stormwatch's lap, and his ears twitched as he raised his head and sniffed the air.

"It all seems like a child's tale! If I may say, Captain, let's just grab the gold and be on our way," said a tall, skinny man in a blue woolen hat who had a long mustache capped at each end with gold beads.

"Listen to me, Kreezer," the captain said in a deep and serious tone. "This is your first run for this terrible gold. It *would* seem like a child's fancy story to a fool like you! But perhaps you would like to be first off-deck to face it?"

McCoy hopped off the captain's lap and made his way towards Rupert.

Kreezer mumbled something, and the captain stood up.

"Wicked spirits guard this gold. This terrible, terrible gold," Captain Stormwatch began, lowering his voice to a whisper. "But an even more wicked spirit has sent us on this quest, and we must wait for his word. Then, and only then, may we leave this vessel and enter the crypt."

Rupert's mind was spinning again. What wicked spirit? A crypt? Why was this gold so terrible?

"That terrible spirit you speak of also wants to put a stop to Winter Joy," said Wurmzy. He scratched the top of his bald head. "How will you face your children when there are no gifts for them under the trinket tree?"

A chorus of confused questions and expressions of shock erupted.

"What do you mean, no more Winter Joy? What sort of rubbish is that! Such a foul and evil demon!"

"Silence!" the captain ordered. "We have been hired to collect the gold. Never have I been told we were helping end the Winter holiday."

"Perhaps," Wurmzy replied, "but we all know what that gold will be used for. It's even more terrible than you think. We'll have the gold. Not even Gripper can stop us if we band together and refuse to just hand it over to him for the few crumbs he's tossing at us."

More talking erupted, and the captain slammed his heavy fist on the tabletop.

"We have our mission, and we will complete it and head back to our homes. Let the evil demons do as they wish."

Rupert felt a soft rub and looked down to see McCoy brushing back and forth against his invisible legs. The cat began his loud purring. Rupert tried to push him gently away, but it only seemed to encourage the friendly kitty even more.

One of the men at the table, a squat man who wore a green-and-yellow shirt and had a snake tattooed around his neck, glanced across the room and spotted McCoy's antics. His eyes opened wider than his mouth. The axe-faced man who sat across from him chuckled.

"What's wrong with you? Look like you just saw the ghost of your old great-grandfather!"

"I think maybe I am seeing a ghost, as I live and breathe! Seems McCoy has made pals with it!"

All heads turned towards Rupert. Of course, no one saw him, just the orange-and-white kitty rubbing up against—nothing!

The captain slowly walked towards McCoy.

"Hey, there, boy, whatcha got? A little mouse, maybe?"

McCoy meowed and purred and made little happy noises. Rupert wanted to run, but he was afraid to move. The captain stepped closer, squinting his eyes as if that might show him what the cat was cozying up to. Very slowly, he extended his index finger closer and closer to Rupert's invisible face.

The finger was less than an inch away when Rupert lunged his head forward and chomped his teeth down on it. Captain Stormwatch screamed and snatched back his throbbing finger as chaos exploded. The captain looked like he wanted to run, but he couldn't. He had to stay strong in front of his men. He grimaced and put his hands on his hips.

"Listen, you foul demon! I order you to leave this vessel!"

Rupert's invisible smile went ear to ear. The captain frowned angrily and, with clenched fists, took another step towards him. Rupert took a deep breath and let out a huge, loud roar that even scared McCoy, who scampered under the table.

The captain got a silly expression, and he jumped back in fear. Many of his man raced out of the room. Rupert was trying not to laugh, and then the captain pulled a large knife from the sheath hanging on his belt. Rupert's smile vanished as he watched the knife rise into the air.

"They are attacking!" one of the crewmen cried.

The captain froze, and Rupert spun around and raced down the hallway and up the stairs to the deck. The moist air hit his face and felt refreshing. The rain had stopped.

There was a sound of clanging metal behind him, and when he turned, he couldn't believe what he saw. Ten skeletons dressed in golden suits of armor were trying to board the boat!

Captain Stormwatch rushed ondeck, a mean-looking sword with a curved blade held out before him. The rest of his crew tumbled out behind him, all with swords, spears, and harpoons at the ready.

"Attack these gilded demons! The heads! Off with their heads!" ordered the captain.

The men rushed the army of skeletons; swords swung, and metal clanged against metal.

Rupert stepped back and was not sure what to do. He watched the captain, with a clean swing of his sword, lop the helmeted skull off one skeleton. The body beneath it collapsed in a lifeless pile of gold. The captain laughed with delight.

But not all his men were as skilled, and two of them had been knocked off their feet and were wrestling with the invaders on the deck. Another was pushed overboard and splashed into the water.

Rupert knew he had to help. If the skeletons defeated the crew, he would be stuck here forever. Maybe he would be discovered by the skeletons and killed!

He closed his eyes and tried to think of something. He didn't realize he was no longer invisible, nor that the glass ball in his jacket pocket was growing even hotter than before.

Rupert felt cold breath on his neck. He was afraid to breath.

"Hello, Master Rupert." Gripper greeted him.

Chapter 17

Over a Barrel

"Such silly men, aren't they, Rupert?"

Rupert turned to face the horrid smile and frigid eyes of Bolton Gripper. He could only manage a meek shrug.

Where had he come from?

"We know what needs to be done, don't we, Rupert? We know silly swords and poles are no match for a potent imagination. An imagination that can create tattle-tale glass balls and render one invisible."

Rupert swallowed hard. He glanced down at his feet and realized the swirling invisibility shield he had Imagined was gone.

"How would you stop those bony ghouls, Rupert?"

"I'm…not…sure…" He was trying to act normal and calm. He was trying to hide his fear in its own swirling mass of invisibility snow.

"I have an idea. Watch and learn, my protégé."

Gripper closed his eyes and placed a fingertip on his temple. Amidst the shouting, clanging and din of the battle, there came the sound of rushing, bubbling water. Over the side of the craft came a fountain of water that twirled like a tornado. From the mouth of its funnel flew bright red fish, each the size of watermelon.

They had ruby-red scales and flat heads. Where their mouths should have been were spinning saw blades that whined and buzzed! Rupert's belly tightened as the sound of the saws reminded him of the piranha birds that had almost shredded him in Far-Myst.

But the fish flew right past him and went after the skeletons. One by one, the fish neatly sliced off the heads, which bounced on the deck like golden basketballs. The suits of armor collapsed like old metal laundry. The crew could only stand stunned.

"Now they will take care of that traitor Wurmzy!" Gripper snarled in a raspy, drooling voice.

Rupert looked all around the deck. Wurmzy was no-where to be seen. He hadn't taken part in the battle and was probably still in the galley. The swarm of red saw-fish gathered and, with a swish, flew down the staircase. There was a terrible scream and then silence.

Rupert shot a steely look of anger at Gripper.

"How could you do that?"

Gripper smiled and patted Rupert's head.

"I think you will have more pressing concerns."

Rupert turned to see the captain storming his way.

"Hey! Where did you come from, boy?" Captain Storm-watch shouted.

Rupert wanted to run but didn't know where he could run to. He looked around and noticed Gripper had van-ished. He swallowed his fear and quickly thought up a lie.

"I got lost. I need a ride back to town."

"So, the stowaway is lost? Needs a ride home?" mocked the captain.

The men laughed.

"Begin collecting the gold! Put it in the barrels!" the captain ordered. "But leave one empty. We must treat our little rodent as a guest! Come here, my lad."

Rupert kicked him in the knee and ran.

"Grab him!" Stormwatch screamed, hopping on one leg and rubbing his throbbing knee.

Crewmen spread out across the deck. Rupert had no choice but to rush down the steps and hope he could find a good hiding spot until he could use his Imaginings.

He raced into the galley and froze. The sight before him was too horrible to look at. The crewmen in rushed behind him.

The lid was slammed shut, and Rupert was in the cozy confines of a barrel. This time there was no McCoy there to comfort him. Slashes of light leaked in from two holes bored in the lid.

At least I have air holes.

He would compose himself and try clear his mind of the image of Wurmzy's terrible fate. Surely, he would be kept in the barrel until they returned and docked on Riverside Road then let go.

The loud clangs of golden armor being dropped into barrels poked at his ears. Then there was silence. A blast from the smokestack, and the movement of the *Hammerhead* announced the return trip had begun.

After twenty minutes or so, Rupert heard two sets of footsteps creaking along the deck. Closer and closer they came. His barrel was tipped, and the sensation of rising into the air filled his belly.

There was a sense of sudden movement, and then a splash. He was bobbing and moving! Distant voices dripping with laugher yelled, "Bon Voyage!"

They threw me overboard! he realized in horror.

Rupert was in a pickle barrel for sure. He wasn't sure what he could do. He still had nightmares from his frightening time on the Frothing River during his adventures in Far-Myst.

He tried to calm his mind.

This is different. I'm floating in a dry boat. A barrel boat. I'm safe. Someone will spot it and rescue me. But what if they don't see it? What if I just float forever? End up in the ocean?

All sorts of not very nice thoughts were filling his mind. He needed to chase those images away. He needed to rake all those ugly leaves off the lawn of his imagination.

It was growing colder. His jacket was warm, but the nighttime winter air was seeping into his bones, making his teeth chatter. He fingered the glass ball in his jacket pocket then took it out. In the darkness of the barrel, he could barely make out the figure of the cat.

That was a good thing. No danger or bad guys in the area. He wished the eyes *would* glow so he would have some more light. Maybe some of the light would leak out of the holes in the lid and make it easier for people to see him from the shore.

What would really be great would be if there were two bright lights attached to the top of the barrel that flashed bright cherry-red and could be seen for miles. There was no reason there couldn't be.

Rupert felt his mind drift like a cork floating on the ocean. His imagination dipped and bobbed, and pictures of a barrel on the surface of the river appeared. He felt like he was slipping into a dream.

He watched as the dark barrel suddenly grew brighter and brighter until it was as red as an apple and bright as a street lamp. The red light flickered like a flame. No, it was more like a steady beat. A pulse. With each beat of his heart, the red light dimmed and brightened.

Rupert slipped deeper into this dream world, and more than an hour passed like water in a stream.

A thud popped Rupert's eyes open. He hadn't even realized they were closed or that he had been dreaming. A strong red light flashed outside, and some of this light leaked in through the two holes, making the lid look like two red eyes stared down at him. He felt the barrel lift into the air.

He dropped down and landed with a soft bounce. Footsteps approached. Rupert was holding the glass ball. It was dark and cool. The lid of the barrel was pried off. Rupert stared up at the face of Ensen Starkey, glowing in bright-red light.

"Well, hello, Mr. Rupert Dullz. Fancy meeting you here," he said with a smile. He reached in and helped Rupert from his makeshift boat.

Rupert couldn't believe it. The barrel was aglow with such a bright-red light it hurt his eyes to look at it.

"Yes, I couldn't believe it either when I saw it floating along. Probably should cover it so as to not attract attention."

Ensen tossed a large canvas sheet over the barrel. Rupert looked around and saw he was aboard a pretty sailboat made of polished wood. The sails were deep blue, and the mast and boom were of polished ebony wood that made them look like solid shadows.

The barrel had been lifted from the water by a rope-and-pulley machine Ensen Starkey was busy securing. He opened his arms wide and smiled.

"Welcome aboard my pride and joy — the *Tall Tale*."

Chapter 18

Golden Tales

Ensen Starkey placed a hot cup of cocoa in front of Rupert, who sat with a comfy blanket around his shoulders.

"That should warm you to the bones." he said, sitting down across the table and sipping from his own cup.

"Thanks, " Rupert said, taking a sniff then a sip. He smiled. "That's really good."

"You know what is really good?" Ensen stopped and studied Rupert, who finally shrugged. "The imagination of a boy who can make a barrel glow like a campfire."

Rupert gulped down his mouthful of cocoa as his face turned red.

"Tell me, Mr. Dullz, how long have you been able to use your Imagining powers?"

Rupert felt nervous talking about his abilities. He really didn't know this man at all.

"I was shoved in that barrel and thrown off a boat. Maybe they made it glow?"

Ensen got up and walked over to a shelf of books. He took out a large one with a red leather cover, placed it on the table, and slid it across to Rupert. The title was *The Island of Terrible Gold*.

Rupert slowly flipped through the book and was surprised to find a colorful illustration of an army of skeletons in golden armor battling pirates.

"I saw these guys! They were trying to take over the boat!" He continued flipping through the pages. The words were all handwritten with blue ink. "Who wrote this?" he asked with growing excitement.

"A friend of mine. A man named Mookie Starbright," Ensen explained. "Look at the last page."

Rupert anxiously turned to the back, and sure enough, at the bottom of the last page, after the words The End, was the signature of Mookie Starbright.

He looked up at Ensen in amazement.

"You know Mookie Starbright?"

"Yes, I do. He has a special ability. He can create stories — imagine them — and they will often come true. This can be good or bad, depending on what he imagines.

"The gold on that island has the power to do either good or evil, depending on the thoughts of who uses it. He wrote this story to protect the special gold. To keep it out of certain hands. Hands of someone who now wants to make terrible changes. I guess the protection was no match for that dark soul."

"Gripper?" Rupert whispered.

Ensen leaned toward him and spoke softly.

"There are people who want to replace all the good things in life — things that are free, things that have real value — with things you have to buy. They hate when people are happy in here." Ensen said tapped his heart. "Or in here." He tapped his forehead.

"Why? Don't they want to be happy, too?"

"Rupert, some people become gold-happy. They forget that what is really valuable is what is in their heart and their mind. They get greedy, and so when they have a lot, they want more. And when they get more, they want even more. Then they want power. They want to control what everybody else wants.

"Some see the Winter Joy as a waste of time. Why, they say, should people *make* gifts for others when they should be spending their money and *buying* gifts? They think it is silly to believe in the spirit of a kind woman who sends her magical cat to reward people for being kind."

"But you have a lot of money. Don't you feel the same way?"

Ensen smiled. "I do have a lot of money. But, no, Rupert, I don't feel that way."

"What about making a law so that people have to buy more of your rakes?"

"There are many things some people want me to do. That's why I have this boat. So I can escape. Get away from that and clear my mind. I spend time with Mookie Starbright, and he reminds me of good things. Like the imagination. Like that special power he has. That you have."

"Where does Mookie live?"

"I promised I would keep that a secret." Ensen looked at Rupert curiously. "How do *you* know about Mookie Starbright?"

Rupert wasn't sure how to answer the question. He chose his words carefully.

"My grandmother told me about him. Not sure how she knew. She said he wrote just-because stories."

"Do you write just-because stories, too?"

"No. But…"

Rupert thought about explaining to Ensen about Pie O'Sky and the door to Far-Myst, but he still wasn't sure he could trust him. He *seemed* nice, but he *was* friends with that creepy Gripper guy.

Instead, he took the globe from his pocket and set it on the table. Ensen leaned closer to study the cat within. He looked up at Rupert.

"Did you Imagine this?"

Rupert nodded. Ensen smiled wider, amazement on his face. He paced a bit then turned to face him.

"Rupert, my boy, perhaps I *can* tell you – "

A glow of red light pooled on the table around the globe as the cat's eyes lit up.

"Why is it doing that?" Ensen asked.

"It means there's danger close," Rupert told him, looking around the cabin nervously.

A grey mist seeped in through the spaces around the door. It came together to make two skeletal hands, and then a horrible face formed in the wood of the door. The boat rocked.

"Gripper," Rupert whispered.

"Don't look at it, Rupert," Ensen murmured then glared at the specter. "Leave my craft at once!"

The boat rocked and rolled even more, knocking Ensen off-balance and sending the globe rolling across the table. Ensen was quick as a cat, diving to catch it before it crashed to the floor.

The ghostly fingers became gray flames that sparked and then flashed orange. With a terrible swipe, they set the walls of the cabin ablaze! A wall of fire blocked the only way to escape. Black smoke filled the room.

Ensen grabbed Rupert by the arm.

"Can you swim?"

"No!"

Ensen looked around then rushed to a small closet. From the shelf inside, he grabbed a blanket and, with a flip, unfolded it. He threw it over his head and pulled Rupert under with him.

"Stay close. we're going to run out the door and onto the deck. Ready?"

"Okay."

"Run!"

They raced across the cabin, right through the wall of fire, out the door and up the steps onto the deck. Ensen flung away the blanket, which had caught fire and was quickly burning up. He checked Rupert.

"You okay?"

"Yeah, I think so." Rupert coughed and tried to get a good lungful of fresh air.

Smoke was pouring out from below. Ensen looked across at the shore. The *Tall Tale* would be engulfed in fire very soon. It was too far to risk sailing.

"We're going to have to abandon ship and swim to shore," he told Rupert.

"But I can't—"

"You'll ride on my back."

He knelt so Rupert could put arms around his neck and legs around his waist then stood up, wobbled a bit, and went to the railing. The flames were now eating through the decking. Thick, billowing clouds of smoke rose. With a flash, the mainsail exploded in flames.

"Hold on tight!" Ensen shouted.

He dove off the *Tall Tale* and into the cold water of the river.

Chapter 19

Fire and Water

The water was like ice, bone-numbingly cold. Rupert felt the heat of the burning boat on his back, but even that wasn't enough to hold back the shivers rattling his entire body. Smelly smoke wafted all around them and made it even more difficult to breath.

Ensen was swimming with all his strength, and Rupert heard him struggling to breathe. He wished he had learned to swim so Ensen didn't have to work so hard to rescue them both.

His memories of being washed into the Frothing River in Far-Myst were still fresh in his mind, and he'd had a few nightmares about it since. He had promised himself he would ask his father to teach him how to swim, but at the same time he was afraid to discuss those dangerous adventures with his dad.

He just hoped Ensen had the strength to make it to safety.

Little by little, the smoke began to clear as Ensen got closer to the shore. Rupert tossed a glance over his shoulder and was saddened at the sight. The entire boat was in flames, and it was sinking.

There was nothing to be seen but forest lining the river, although he could see the lights of Gracelandville in the distance. They were not too far from where the *Hammerhead* had left the dock.

"Is...she...a... goner?" Ensen asked. Each word was a struggle to speak.

"Don't worry about the boat. Let's get to shore!" Rupert said with chattering teeth.

He could tell the cold was wearing Ensen out. If only he could fight on for a few more minutes. They were so close, yet so far. He looked back at the burning *Tall Tale*. His mouth fell open.

"Ho-lee mo-lee!"

Shapes were forming in the flames—fiery birds with blazing outspread wings. One by one, they took to the air and dove into the water. Rupert could see them glowing beneath the surface, heading toward them.

"We have another problem!" he yelled.

"What?"

"I'm not sure yet." He had no clue what the fiery birds would do.

Five more were born in the flames and dove into the river. He had to think. He had to Imagine. Fast!

Rupert was cold and wet, and he wished he could be warm and dry like the cat inside the glass ball.

Inside the ball!

He smiled to himself and ignored the fiery birds closing in on them. He Imagined a giant bubble, like the soap bubble that would sometimes pop out of his shampoo bottle when he squeezed it. The bubble would grow around them, but it would be made of solid glass. Glass that would be —

Ensen let out a sudden scream.

"What's wrong?" Rupert asked.

"My feet! Something burned my feet!"

Rupert looked. The firebird-fish were on them.

He closed his eyes and ignored the searing heat. Ensen yelled again in pain.

"Rupert! You have to Imagine some help!"

"I am! Just keep swimming and leave the Imagining to me!"

He focused on creating the giant glass ball. He watched the sphere grow in his mind and smiled as it became so clear he felt he could reach out and touch it. He opened his eyes and noticed the shoreline seemed warped. He reached out one hand. He felt glass!

"I did it!"

Before Ensen could reply, they began sinking under the water. The glass ball was all around them, but Rupert had overlooked one small detail — the bottom half was filled with river water. The weight acted like an anchor.

They bounced on the bottom. Ensen stood, the trapped water up to his knees. It was up to Rupert's waist. They watched the firebird-fish bounce harmlessly off the outside of the ball.

"You did it, Rupert!" Ensen shouted, desperately trying to catch his breath. "You have an amazing ability, my boy. Mookie Starbright would approve."

"But now we're trapped in here on the bottom of the river," Rupert pointed out, growing panicky.

"One step at a time. We'll push this ball to the shore like a hamster on an exercise wheel!"

Rupert nodded and smiled.

"Like *two* hamsters!"

They pushed with all their might, but the weight of the water was too much. The glass bubble didn't budge an inch.

"Keep pushing, Rupert!"

They struggled and strained but only managed to make the water slosh around.

"Think there's enough air in here?" Rupert asked.

"I'm sure there..." Ensen looked upward. "Hear that?"

Rupert looked up, too, and his eyes widened.

"Stand back—and hold your breath!" Ensen yelled. He pushed Rupert out of harm's way as something crashed through the globe in a shower of glass and water.

Chapter 20

An Unexpected Detour

An anchor rope hung before them. Ensen smiled and motioned for Rupert to climb it. Rupert struggled to hold his breath as fought his way up. His head broke the surface, and he gasped for air.

Jethro the butler stared at him from a small rowboat.

He helped Rupert into the boat. A few seconds later, Ensen reached the surface and joined them. Jethro had a few large blankets, and he wrapped Rupert in one while Ensen helped himself.

"Jethro, remind me to raise your salary," Ensen said. "Are you okay, Rupert?"

Rupert nodded and turned to Jethro.

"How did you know where to find us, Mr. Jethro?"

Jethro handed him a cup of hot tea from a thermos and began pouring a second.

"I was on Crimson Alley pier waiting for Mr. Starkey when I saw the terrible fire. I rowed out just in time to see that rather odd glass sphere form from thin air and sink under the surface. I am thankful I had a large enough anchor and a long enough rope."

"As are we," Ensen Starkey said with a shiver in his voice. "Let's get home."

Jethro grabbed the oars and rowed toward the pier.

Rupert and Ensen sat in the comfortable horse-drawn coach as Jethro drove along the quiet nighttime roads to Gracelandville. Their clothes were still soaked, so the warmth of the blankets and the shelter of the vehicle's plush interior felt great.

Rupert's thoughts drifted to his home in the future. He hoped his parents weren't worried sick about him, and that Squeem was safe. Was the big bell from the town square in Ensen's rundown house there? If it was, had the firemen found it when they put out the fire? Did they ring it? What would happen if they did? If he could stop the bell from being moved would that change the future?

It was all so confusing.

He did know one of the evil golden bells was loose in Gracelandville, in the hands of the fish seller, given to him by Wurmzey, who was now dead aboard the *Hammerhead*. Rupert tried to shake the image of the buzzsaw fish doing their bloody deed.

He wondered what would happen if the fish seller rang the bell. Would it summon the terrible spider-creatures?

"Can I ask you something, Mr. Ensen?"

"Of course, Rupert."

"What will happen if the bells get covered in gold?"

"That gold is special, Imagined by Mookie Starbright. No one was meant to find it. It was just a story about a magical gold that could make your dreams come true.

"When Gripper realized its power — and that it actually existed — he understood it could also make your *nightmares* come true. He saw a perfect answer to his hatred of Winter Joy. If he could coat the gildens with this terrible magical gold, when folks rang them they would bring terror and not joy."

"But he works for you. Can't you just fire him?"

Ensen smiled in a way that wasn't happy and shook his head.

"It's much more complicated. Much more. But thank goodness, none of the bells has been distributed."

"One has," Rupert told him.

"What do you mean?" Ensen said, sitting up.

"I saw this bald man with an eye patch give the fish man one of the bells."

"When?"

"This morning." It felt like it had happened a week ago.

"Jethro!" Ensen shouted.

"Yes, sir?"

"We need to make a stop. The Hook in Water at once!"

"Yes, sir."

Twenty minutes later, Jethro brought the horses to a halt outside the Hook in Water. The street outside Brooch's store was empty. All the shops were closed, and only a breeze and a scattering of leaves traveled across the cobblestones. Light poured from the front window of the fish store.

"Wait here, Rupert," Ensen said, exiting the coach.

Rupert watched him approach the shop, and his curiosity was too strong. He quietly exited and followed.

Ensen turned the knob on the door and found it unlocked. He pushed it open and called out, "Brooch? You here?"

He stepped inside. Rupert was right behind him. Ensen was staring, mouth agape, at the undersea mural. Rupert looked up and wasn't sure what was holding Ensen's attention in its grip.

"What's wrong?" he asked.

"This painting. Mookie Starbright painted it. There is something *very* wrong."

Rupert scanned the colorful painting from side to side and top to bottom. There they were in their glory: the sharks, barracudas, sawfish, hammerheads, and swordfish. The redfish, bluefish, purplefish, and yellowfish were all there.

Yet there *was* something missing.

"The octopus! Where is it?"

"That's a good question," Ensen said softly.

Rupert took a step. There was a little tinkling sound at his feet. He looked down, and there it was — a golden gilden lying on the floor.

A horrible stream of gooey water trailed across the shop and through a doorway in the rear.

"Look," he said, pointing.

Ensen took a large apron from a shelf and used it to pick up the bell. He wrapped it up tightly to muffle any ringing. He then walked slowly towards the doorway to the back room, following but taking care not to step on the wet goop.

"Stay where you are, Rupert."

Ensen reached the doorway. He cautiously peered in.

"Poor Brooch," he said sadly.

"What happened?"

"We better leave and call — "

"Look out!" Rupert shouted.

Two large tentacles rose from behind the counter and swiped at Ensen's head. Three more appeared, and one slithered around his waist. He knocked one of them away with his fist, but the one gripping his body held tight.

"Rupert! Get out of here!" he cried.

Rupert didn't leave. Instead, he looked around the room and spotted a fishing pole hanging on the wall. He grabbed it and swatted the tentacles as hard as he could. Another arm rose and wrapped around the pole, and Rupert found himself in a tug of war with the creature.

The monster was strong, and Rupert's strength was draining away. Another slippery arm slithered around his waist, and he felt his body moving closer and closer to the horrible head of the octopus.

"I can't get loose!"

"Can you reach that big knife hanging on the wall?" Ensen shouted.

Rupert looked around again and finally spotted the big blade hanging from a hook behind the counter. It was too far away.

"No!"

Ensen tried to stretch his free arm with all his might, but his hand was still a good foot away from the weapon. Another tentacle sprang into action and took hold of the free hand.

"I need to Imagine something!" Rupert cried yelled. "Something that scares octopuses!"

"Great idea, Rupert! Eels!"

"Eels?"

"Eels eat octopods! Can you imagine an eel?"

Rupert was about to close his eyes and try when his entire body was yanked closer to the open mouth of the beast.

"He's gonna eat me!"

"Imagine, Rupert!"

Something caught Rupert's attention on the other side of the store, and he smiled with relief.

"Mr. Jethro!"

"What are you doing, Rupert?" Ensen tried to kick the octopus with his partially free leg.

"Call Mr. Jethro!"

"Why?"

"Just do it!"

"Jethro!" Ensen shouted.

The front door bells rang, and Jethro rushed in.

"Oh, my!" he cried, staring in shock.

"Mr. Jethro—an eel! Throw me one of those eels!" Rupert ordered.

Jethro turned to the ice-filled tray of long, fat eels. He grimaced.

"You want me to touch one of these foul things?"

"Yes! Throw it at the octopus!"

"Ugh," Jethro mumbled, but he picked up one of the eels with the tips of his fingers and tossed it. It landed on Rupert's feet.

"Harder! Throw it harder, and hit the octopus, not me!" Rupert shouted.

A tentacle reached out and slapped Jethro, leaving a slimy splotch on his angered face. Jethro grabbed a large eel and threw it as hard as he could at the octopus's face. The octopus shuddered.

"Great! Another one!" Rupert yelled.

A longer eel flew through the air and landed across the face of the eight-armed beast. The octopus shuddered again, and this time it pulled back some of its arms, including the ones wrapped around Ensen's arms.

"Great! Another, Jethro! Another!"

Eels were flying like slimy arrows. One after another, the snake-like fish bombarded the octopus, which squealed in horror and wrapped all eight limbs around its face like a child hiding their eyes from a scary movie. Rupert was free.

113

"It worked!"

"Good job, Jethro! Let's go, Rupert!" Ensen grabbed the gilden wrapped in the apron and guided Rupert and Jethro out the front door. The bells above the door rang as it slammed.

The horse and buggy was back on the road. Rupert and Ensen sat without saying anything for a moment, catching their breath and relaxing for the first time in a long while. Ensen had the gilden, still wrapped in the apron, sitting on his lap.

Rupert knew that somehow one of the little gildens would end up buried in his yard. He felt like he needed to tell Ensen. He just wasn't sure how.

"How do you know that more bells aren't already out there? Maybe Gripper already gave some away," Rupert wondered.

"Gripper never gives anything away. If he has a heart its made of money," Ensen said with a frown. "Truth is, I don't know for sure. I know he had plans to make Winter Joy more profitable for my business, but until tonight, I didn't realize how far he was willing to go."

Rupert looked at Ensen Starkey. He seemed like such a nice man. Not someone who hurt people for money. Who would want to do such terrible things?

"Can I ask you something?" he asked softly.

"Of course."

"Why do you do business with Gripper?"

Ensen smiled at the question then took a deep breath and exhaled hard.

"That is a very wise question with a very complicated answer. Let's just say I didn't realize who Gripper was when we met. He wanted to help build my tool business, make it more profitable, but there was more to it. It's not like I can just fire him."

114

"Why not?"

"It's complicated."

"My father always says if you planted the tree then you rake up its leaves."

"That's very quaint advice," Ensen said, rolling his eyes. "But it really is more complicated."

"But he tried to kill us! He burned your boat. You can't just let him boss you around!" Rupert said very firmly.

"This is of no concern to a child!" Ensen looked very angry

"Yes, it is! Winter Joy makes all the kids happy!"

"I will do whatever I have to do! As for you, young man who knows it all, you will go to bed, and in the morning, I will see to it you are returned to your home!"

"Well, good luck with that!" snapped Rupert. He bit his lip and stared out the window.

Ensen retrieved the glass globe from his pocket and looked at the cat inside. He held it out to Rupert.

"Here's your globe. I'm sure you never want to lose it." His voice had softened.

Rupert took it back and nodded.

"You need a good night's sleep," Ensen said.

"If you planted the tree then you rake up its leaves," Rupert muttered to himself.

Chapter 21

A Ghostly, Ghastly Secret

Jethro found a change of clothes for Rupert and sent him and a small meal upstairs to his temporary bedroom. Rupert was exhausted. Not since the days hiking through the Wildness of Far-Myst with Dream Weaver had he felt so tired.

As he sat eating thick and hearty chicken soup, he thought about Pie O'Sky. There had to be a good reason Pie O'Sky had created the door for him to travel back to old-time Graysland.

The door to Far-Myst had taken him to a wonderful place that needed the help of his Imaginings. He had helped to change the wicked Murkus's heart and return the children of Far-Myst to their families along with the wondrous colors that made the place sparkle.

Well, Gracelandville was in trouble as well. Did Pie O'Sky expect Rupert to help save Winter Joy from a dangerous and cold-hearted man like Gripper? A man who seemed to have strong Imagining powers of his own. Was Rupert supposed to change history?

Why hadn't Pie O'Sky explained it? Why didn't he sing a fun song like he had that special night when he first appeared over Graysland in his Grand Bagoon?

Voices interrupted his thoughts. He recognized Ensen and Gripper, talking downstairs, their voices coming from a vent in the floor. He knelt and put his ear closer to it to listen, but the words were too muffled. He tiptoed to the door and slipped out quietly into the hallway.

He crept to the top of the stairs and peered down. He could see Ensen pacing while Gripper sat on a sofa.

"I am done with you," Ensen said angrily. "You crossed the line when you put that child in danger!"

"That boy has Imagining abilities to rival the both of us. He might prove quite valuable for business."

"Our business is done. I am through. I am selling the company, and my days with you are over."

"Is that a fact? And how do suppose I will allow that to happen? Do you forget that I exist because of you?"

"What good does all this money do a ghost? You can't spend it. You help no one. What good does it do you?"

A *ghost*?

"It's not about the money, Ensen. It's about power. Something I never had in life, but which you gave me in death. You Imagined it for me."

"I regret that. But I can Imagine much more."

Gripper laughed loud and mockingly and stood up. He glanced toward where Rupert was hiding, and Rupert ducked into the shadows.

Ensen has Imagining powers, too? If he did, why would he waste them on a creepo like Gripper?

"You can try to imagine whatever you wish, my dear Mr. Starkey, but we *will* turn Winter Joy into a profitable holiday. We will strike fear into the people, and they will do whatever we ask of them. Power, my friend. We will have it whether you want it or not."

Gripper then dissolved into a swirl of smoke.

Rupert's mouth fell open. *He* is *a ghost!* he thought in amazement. He rushed back to his room and closed the door.

He paced back and forth nervously. *A ghost – Gripper is the ghost Folky mentioned. Does she know the ghost's identity?*

It did make sense. Gripper always seemed to appear and vanish without warning. What had Ensen done to bring him back from dead? Every question seemed to split and pop into more questions. He wished he could talk to Pie O'Sky.

Rupert closed his eyes and tried to Imagine the bagoon was floating outside the window. He tried to draw a detailed picture in his mind of its brilliant colors. Surely, if he Imagined hard enough, Pie O'Sky would come and answer the questions.

The picture was now clear in his mind, so clear he could feel the wind in his hair as he soared among the clouds!

Rupert opened his eyes. He wanted to laugh. Hanging in the air before him was a tiny version of the Grand Bagoon not much bigger than his own head. He smiled and stepped closer to it to peer into the gondola, but it was empty. There was no tiny version of Pie O'Sky.

A sudden red glow caught his attention. The cat's eyes in the glass ball, which he'd set on the nightstand, were beaming. He shot his attention back to the mini-bagoon, and it changed in a that instant to the face of Gripper!

Rupert jumped back as the face screamed silently. All the skin melted away and left just a skull. He hid his eyes.

A cold hand fell onto his shoulder, and he almost forgot to breathe! When he turned, Gripper was there, his face twisted in a nasty smile.

"Are you frightened of me, Rupert?"

Rupert swallowed and shook his head no.

"You should be," Gripper hissed. "Your friend is still in danger, you know."

"I saw Squeem run. He ran home. I saw him!"

With a great sweep of his arms, Gripper produced a blast of black smoke that formed a large ball. Light flickered within it, and a scene appeared—a room with a large wooden crate, a small oil lamp and a single oval red-glass window. Sitting on top of the crate was Squeem. He looked lonely. And scared.

"Squeem," Rupert said softly. He shot a hard look at Gripper. "But he got away, and the house burned down! How can he be there?"

"It did not burn down," Gripper chuckled. "Don't you think a man with Imagining powers like mine can blow out even a blazing inferno like this!" He snapped his fingers.

"You're not gonna hurt him, are you?"

"So long as you do not interfere with my plan. Tomorrow night is the eve of Winter Joy, and the good folks of Gracelandville will gather in the town square to ring their gildens. My golden gildens." Gripper leaned closer, and Rupert felt the cold touch of his breath. "Winter Joy will become a winter horror. You will not get in my way, and then—maybe—I will free your friend."

Rupert stared into his cold eyes.

"Why are you so unhappy?" he asked.

"Unhappy? I have never been happier!"

"But you're a...ghost. How could you be a ghost and need money?"

"It's not about money, my boy.

119

"I knew a man like you. He wanted it to be dull and boring and scary for everybody. It was all because his baby was dead. He was sad and forgot how to be happy."

Gripper's face tightened.

"What happened that made you so unhappy?"

Gripper's face grew large and skull-like. He howled with anger. His body turned into bright-green fire, and he vanished in a flash. Rupert was left staring at empty space, his heart pounding hard.

"So, I'm really sorry I dropped some of the fergooder gifts. It was an accident, and I'll do whatever I have to make it up," Rupert said sincerely to Sara, who was busy preparing a tray of cupcakes.

He yawned. He hadn't had a good night's sleep. Images of skulls and Gripper's terrible face kept popping into his dreams. He yawned again.

Folky stood by with a smirk on her face.

"You are such a klutso, Dullz," she said with a chuckle.

"Folka, that's not nice," Folky's mom said as she placed the pan into the oven. "Anyone can trip while trying to save a cat from getting run over by a fishmonger's wagon. Why don't you feed your birds and then get Rupert some breakfast. And then, Rupert, I really think it's time you get back home. Your parents are surely worried sick by now!"

"Yes, Mrs. Tweenbort."

"Come on, Rupert," Folky grabbed him by the hand and pulled him from the kitchen.

He watched as she placed handfuls of seeds and breadcrumbs into the cages. He studied her face. It was so odd knowing that this spunky young girl would grow up to be the sweet old lady he knew and loved.

"Hey, Folky, do you ever cough?"

"Cough? That's a weird question."

"No, it ain't. I'm just asking. My grandmother has something called the coffus."

"One time I had a bad cold. Was coughing and sneezing, and I had a temp'ture of, like, a hundred and fifty degrees. Stayed home from school for three days. Never get sick too much. Wish I did so I could stay home and play with my birds."

"Can I tell you a secret?"

Folky turned and her face lit up. She nodded excitedly.

"I saw the ghost last night."

"That's no secret. I hear that ghost all the time." She turned back to her birds.

"I said I *saw* him! Not heard. I know who he is."

"Who?"

Rupert whispered the name as softly as he could.

"Gripper."

Folky laughed.

"It's true."

"Gripper? He's Mr. Starkey's business partner!" Folky said with a chuckle.

"Let me tell you a story." Rupert said.

Rupert told her the real story about his adventure in the bell factory. And about the fishmonger, and Wurmzy with the eye patch.

He explained why he had dropped the fergooder gifts and about sneaking aboard the *Hammerhead*. Folky smiled when she heard about McCoy and laughed when he mimed how he'd bitten the captain's finger.

The golden armored skeletons and Gripper's terrible sawfish—she gasped when he told her about Wurmzy's head getting sliced off his neck, and how they had tossed *him* overboard in a barrel. The rescue. The fire. The giant glass ball. The octopus that killed the poor fish seller.

He then told her about Gripper's argument with Ensen the night before, and Gripper's frightening visit to his room.

Folky's mouth hung open during the entire story.

"Do you believe me?" Rupert asked when he was done.

"And my mother says *I* have a wild imagination."

"Its all true. And there's something else."

"What?"

"I'm not from around here. I mean, I am from around here but not now. Not this time. I come from the future. When I live there is no more Winter Joy. Trouble is, my best friend Squeem is in trouble from Gripper, but in the future. Gripper is a ghost, so he can go back and forth. I need a special door to get back."

"Where you gonna get a door like that?"

"A good friend of mine. Name is Pie O'Sky. But what's important right now is that Gripper is going to end Winter Joy with his terrible bells."

"Why would he want to do that?"

"He was mad — or sad — when he was alive. Then Mr. Ensen helped to make him a ghost. Now he wants to be powerful."

"How could Mr. Ensen make a dead man a ghost?"

"He has Imagining powers. Like Gripper has. Like I have."

"You? What kind of imagining did you do?" Folky was doubtful.

"I told you. I made myself invisible, and the barrel glow, and the big glass ball. And this."

Rupert took the glass globe from his pocket and handed it to Folky. She looked at it and shrugged.

"I've seen tons of those at Mrs. Oldman's shop in town. She even has one with a tree, and when you shake it the leaves float around in the water."

"I didn't get this from some dumb shop. I Imagined it. The cat's eyes glow red if danger is around."

Folky still looked doubtful.

"I bet you have Imagining powers, too," Rupert told her.

"Of course I do!" she said proudly.

"Okay, let's see what you can do. What would you like to Imagine?"

Folky thought for a moment then took one of the birds from the cage and held it perched on the side of her hand. He was a pretty green parakeet, and he fluttered his wings and tweeted.

"I want to Imagine that Gypsy will grow big enough so I can ride him and fly around town."

"Okay. Close your eyes and Imagine it. Don't just think about it. See it. Feel the wind blowing your hair when you're flying. "

Folky closed her eyes and smiled as the thoughts filled her head.

"What do you see?"

"Just a bunch of colorful dots," she said frowning.

"Make the dots come together and make a big green bird!"

"I'm trying. Okay, I sort of see a bird. No. It's an apple. I think — "

"Don't think. Just see," Rupert ordered.

"Forget it. This is dumb!" Folky said, frustrated. Her expression changed. "Hey, the cat's eyes are red."

Rupert looked at the globe in his hand. She was right. The eyes were glowing, and the glass was hot. he looked around.

"Maybe Gripper is near," he whispered.

There was a knock on the door. They both gasped but then burst into laughter. Folky opened the door. Ensen stood outside holding a newspaper.

"Hello, children. I wanted to make sure you rake the lawn before you go about your Winter Joy preparations. A new law was passed."

He held out the newspaper to Folky, who took it. The headline read: *RAKE LAW PASSES*.

"Rake law?" she said distastefully. She handed the paper to Rupert.

"That's right," Ensen said. "Every homeowner must keep their lawn free of leaves or risk heavy fines and or imprisonment for repeat offenses. Make sure you use the new rake and have Rupert help. I will be out running some business errands."

He walked off. Rupert watched as the eyes of the cat dimmed.

"I guess today is Graysland's birthday," he said to himself, scanning the paper. Something else caught his attention. "Hey, look at this!" He began reading. "'Get your free gold gilden for Winter Joy. The first five hundred folk who show up for the Eve of Winter's Joy gathering will receive the bell courtesy of E.S., Inc.'"

"So what? Free bells sound great!"

"Bells that will ruin Winter Joy."

Folky rolled her eyes and returned Gypsy to his cage.

"Let's get raking, you kookadoo."

Chapter 22

The Red Glass Room

Rupert and Folky got to work raking the broad lawns of Ensen's mansion. As they worked, his thoughts kept drifting back to Ensen and the cat globe. Why had the cat's eyes turned red when Ensen had appeared at the door? He also thought a lot about his friend. Was Gripper lying, or was Squeem actually being held prisoner?

He scanned the front of the building, searching for the red-glass window. It wasn't on this side of the house. He casually circled all the way around but didn't find it.

"Hey, Rupert. We're done," Folky called.

Rupert looked up at the sky and wished Pie O'Sky's bagoon would appear. There was nothing but big puffy clouds and a few birds.

Rupert spent the day giving out more fergooder gifts. As they walked around town, he whispered about the evil bells of Gripper and how he and Folky needed to stop them from being distributed. Folky still looked at him as if he were nuts.

When they passed the Hook in Water Fish Shop. the door was closed and the lights were out. A large wreath of flowers hung on the door. All the chitter and chatter around the square was that old Brooch had died of natural causes from working such long hours.

Rupert told Folky how the octopus had come out of Mookie's painting. When she laughed, he took her by the hand and led her to the shop so they could peer through the big front window. There was no sign of the octopus in the mural.

"See? It's gone! I told you," he said.

Folky studied the painting, and her face went white.

"That is so creepy," she mumbled. "I thought you were a kookadoo, but there *was* a big octopus in that picture! Where did it go?"

"Just like I told you. It came out and killed the fish man. Then me, Mr. Ensen and Jethro fought it off with frozen eels!"

Folky shook her head and looked him in the eyes.

"Maybe something really weird is going on after all."

Later that afternoon, Rupert helped Folky, Sara and Jethro decorate the big elderpine on the front lawn that would be the trinket tree for Winter Joy. He smiled as each seashell, coin, piece of jewelry, polished stone and strand of ribbons and popcorn were placed on the tree. Jethro added a long green wire lined with glass bulbs shaped like different kinds of fruit.

It seemed odd to him at first, putting all these baubles and bits on the evergreen branches. Yet, when they were done, the tree glistened in the red light of the setting sun and looked beautiful.

Rupert had noticed Jethro tossing looks at the front driveway as they decorated the tree. The coach was gone, and they hadn't seen Ensen all day. Sara noticed it as well.

"Jethro, isn't it odd for Mr. Starkey to not be here to help decorate the tree? It's one of his favorite nights."

"Yes, it is. However, I understand Mr. Starchy had some pressing business in town all day. I am sure he will join us in the square for the ringing of the Winter Joy Eve bells."

"I think something happened to Mr. Ensen," Rupert whispered to Folky.

Jethro had a faraway look in his eyes and a worried expression on his face. The sound of horses' hooves approaching changed that expression, and he relaxed and smiled.

"Ah, here he is now," he said as the coach came to a stop in the driveway. Ensen stepped down from the driver's seat.

Rupert felt a jab of heat in his pocket. He casually slid his hand into his jacket and could feel the globe was hot. He kept a close eye on Ensen.

"Welcome home, sir," Jethro greeted him. "You have arrived just in time to see the trinket tree's lights come to life."

He jogged over to a wooden pole with a metal box attached to it. The other end of the green wire dangled from the box. Jethro took hold of a large switch.

"There's something weird about Mr. Ensen," Rupert whispered to Folky.

"Why?"

"Just watch him."

"Ready?" Jethro called out.

"Let the trinket tree shine like Aranthal in the sky!" Folky and her mother called out on cue. Rupert, not aware of the tradition, just watched silently.

Jethro flicked the switch, and the tree burst into a dazzling display of rainbow fruit.

"Wow!" Rupert exclaimed.

Then he saw something really strange. Ensen's face flickered as the lights came on. It was just for a second, but the man's handsome face changed to the bony and wrinkled one of Gripper.

"Ah. Charming," Ensen said.

"What a lovely tree! As always!" Folky's mom said. "Children, are your gildens ready for tonight?"

"Actually, I have a surprise," Ensen said, removing an object from his coat.

It was wrapped in a deep-blue silk cloth. As he unfolded the silk, the glimmer of gold sparkled. Inside were two golden bells.

"Oh, my! How lovely!" Sara said.

Ensen held the two bells out to Rupert and Folky. Folky smiled and took one.

"Don't ring it until the proper time in the Square. Bad luck for early ringers!" Ensen reminded her.

Rupert just stared him in the eyes. Eyes he knew were Gripper's.

"Here you are, my boy. One for you, as well. You are my guest, after all," Ensen said with a toothy smile.

"Thank you, Mr. Ensen."

He took the bell, carefully putting his fingers around the handle *and* the ringer to keep it from striking. He had made that mistake once. He wasn't going to ring one of these bells with its haunted gold again.

"Well. The trinket tree is lit, and the gildens are ready. Let's feast on a lovely Winter Joy Eve meal, and then we'll be off to the Square!" Jethro said.

"Yes, Jethro. This will be a special night, indeed!"

The adults went into the house, but Rupert held Folky back.

"Let's go, Rupert. I'm starving!" she protested.

"I have to tell you something."

"What?" Folky headed toward the door.

"That's not Mr. Ensen."

She stopped and spun around.

"What kookiness are you talking about now?"

Rupert stepped closer and kept his voice low.

"Did you see? His face changed. It was so creepy. It's Gripper."

"Gripper? But how…?"

"I told you—he's a ghost. I saw him just disappear. He and Mr. Ensen were arguing. I think Mr. Ensen is in trouble."

Folky rolled her eyes.

"If we ring those bells," Rupert continued, "we'll all be in trouble. Like the fish man."

"How can bells make bad things happen?"

"I think they make things that scare you come true. Like the Darkledroons."

"The what?"

"When I rang the bell once before," Rupert said, ignoring her question, "these giant scary spider-dogs appeared."

"You're afraid of spiders? I think they're great!"

"I got bitten by a spider one time, and my hand blew up like a balloon. If everybody rings these bells tonight then everything that scares everybody will appear. It'll be crazy! No one will ever wanna celebrate Winter Joy again."

He must have sounded sincere, because Folky lost her mocking smile. Then, she shook her head and turned to leave.

"What are *you* afraid of, Folky?"

She thought for a moment, and her face went through a bunch of different expressions.

"Dying of hunger! I'm gonna go eat," she said as she raced to the door. "Come join us if you want. You can tell my mom all your crazy stories."

Rupert frowned as she vanished inside.

A crow cawed overhead. He watched the large black bird sail over the yard and land on the big elm that stood at one side of the house. Then he spotted it—something he'd missed before.

At the very top peak of the roof, partially covered by the elm's overhanging leaves and branches, was an oval window. An oval window of red glass.

Rupert made sure all was clear and began climbing the drainpipe up the corner of the house. The red-glass window was high, just below the widow's walk. There was no ledge leading up to it.

There was the elm, though, and Rupert was able to grab hold of a large branch. He climbed until he could see into the room on the other side of the red glass window. The room was dark.

His ears perked up at the sound of horses approaching. A rickety delivery wagon pulled by two old and tired nags pulled into the drive. Two men and a child dressed in black hooded cloaks jumped from the back.

Rupert studied the child and realized it was no child at all but the little person he had seen in the bell factory.

With some struggle, the two big men removed a large wooden crate and carried it to the rear of the house. The little person led the way. After a few minutes, a light came on in the room with the red glass window as the little man entered holding a flaming lantern he set down on a table. The crate was placed on the floor. They all left the room just as quickly as they had entered.

Rupert's mind was racing. Only one thing could be in the box—the bell from the square—but he had to see for himself.

He climbed down from the tree, sneaked around to the back door, and tested the knob. It was unlocked. He peered in and listened. All was quiet, so he entered and discovered it a short hallway with a door at other end. He walked on tippy-toes across the creaky wooden floor and put his ear against the door. It felt cold. Silence lay beyond it.

He opened it and discovered another spiraling staircase. He began climbing. It was dark. Even darker than the secret steps Folky had shown him that led to the widow's walk. He brushed his hand along the walls, which were smooth as marble and very cold. He felt like he was climbing forever.

Then his worst fear happened. He heard three sets of feet descending the steps towards him! Muffled voices joined the footsteps. He could feel the heat of the globe in his pocket.

Light. The light from the cat's eyes might offer some help. He retrieved the ball, and the soft red glow fell on a horrid face that stared right at him! Rupert was sure his heart was going to shoot out of his eyes.

It was just a freaky-looking statue—a gargoyle with folded wings and a wicked grin seated in an alcove carved into the wall.

The footsteps grew closer and the voices clearer. One of the men was complaining about how difficult the steps were to climb and that they should be paid more for their efforts. Rupert had to move or be caught.

He shoved the globe back into his jacket, and the pitch blackness returned. Then he did the only thing he could think of. He climbed into the alcove and sat on the shoulders of the gargoyle.

"What about the other crate?" one of the men asked.

"We have to wait until we get his orders." replied another.

"What about our bellies? Haven't eaten a lousy crumb since breakfast!" said a third voice Rupert recognized as the little man's.

"Your little belly can wait like ours!"

Rupert wished they hadn't mentioned food. He was hungry as well, and he could feel his stomach rumbling. He felt a gas bubble rising into his mouth. This could only mean one thing. A belch was coming, and it was gonna be a good one.

Rupert smelled terrible body odor as the three men came closer. He was battling to hold back the burp that was just behind his tonsils. Maybe he could let out a tiny bit? No. He had to hold it.

As the men passed him, the stink was too great, and his stomach clenched. He tried his best, but a little bubble of belch slipped out of his mouth.

Burp.

The footsteps stopped — just below the alcove.

"You hear that?" one man said.

"Hear what?"

"Not sure."

Rupert dared not move a muscle. The mother of all burps was banging on the back of his throat like an impatient salesman at the front door.

"Would you move your big rump so we can get on with business. It's probably a mouse. This old house is full of them!"

The men continued down the stairs. Their footsteps faded, and the slamming of the door below was music to Rupert's ears.

BUUUUURP!!!

Rupert's belch echoed up and down the staircase. He climbed from the alcove, took a deep breath and ran up the steps. He was breathing hard when he got to the top.

He found a red door. He turned the knob and pushed. It was a heavy door, but it opened smoothly and silently.

The lantern had been left behind and was still burning, and its flicker caused shadows to dance around him. Rupert approached the crate. He wanted to open it, but he didn't know how he could without any tools. He put his ear against the wood and, he wasn't sure why, gently tapped.

To his utter surprise, tapping came from inside!

He jumped away from the box.

"Who's in there?" he asked, ready to run out the door.

"Rupert? Is that you?"

He knew the voice instantly, and a mix of shock and utter happiness filled him. He rushed to the crate.

"Squeem!"

Chapter 23

An Unexpected Visit

"Yes, it's me! Open this stupid box!"

Rupert searched the surface of the crate for a way to open it.

"How? I'll need a crowbar or something."

"There's a latch. It opens like a door," Squeem told him.

Rupert took the lantern and ran its light over the surface of the box until finally there was a twinkle of silver. He smiled and reached for the latch.

There was a creak of wood outside. Then another. The sound of footsteps grew faster as if someone was rushing up the stairs. Rupert scanned the room. He needed another way out.

On the wall just to the right of the red window was a small door. It looked like the pet door at his neighbor Mrs. Pepperpot's, the one her little doberboodle used to go in and out of the house.

"I'll be right back, " he whispered to Squeem.

The small door easily pushed open. Getting on his hands and knees, he slipped through.

He was in a small passageway; he could see dim light at the far end. He was crawling along the cold stone floor when a spider web tickled his face.

His heart raced as he thought of many sets of eight legs crawling over his skin. He tried to clear his mind of his fear. Big ones. Little ones. Red ones. Black ones. Hairy ones. Ones with terrible, poisonous fangs…

He moved his hands and feet as fast as he could, racing to the far end. He learned the light was coming through the grill of a vent where soft moonlight leaked in through the openings. He didn't care about how much noise he might make; he just shoved it as hard as he could, and it fell open with a clang.

He rushed out of the dusty shaft and jumped to his feet in a panic, brushing off his clothes and jumping up and down in disgust.

There were no spiders.

He was in the cupola at the center of the widow's walk; the maze of staircases and hidden passages that lay just below the skin of the house was astounding. He looked out at the town and wasn't sure what to do.

He needed to get back to Squeem and release him from the crate. He also had to get down to dinner, or surely Folky or her mother or, even worse, Gripper/Ensen would come looking for him.

Was it Gripper climbing the steps?

He had to go back, but he hated the idea of crawling through the tunnel with its spiders. Maybe it was just regular old dust.

"If only Pie O'Sky would appear. If only I could talk to him," Rupert muttered.

He closed his eyes and took a deep breath. He smiled to himself. There was something comforting about knowing his best friend was so close. He imagined how nice it would be if Pie O'Sky were close as well.

There was a tapping sound. Rupert opened his eyes and gasped with joy.

"Pie O'Sky!"

The Grand Bagoon was floating just outside the windows over the widow's walk, and the colorful man's smiling face gazed back at him. Rupert scanned the windows for a way to open them and discovered a small latch. He flipped it open and pushed, and with a slight creak, the pane of glass swung open.

"Hello, Rupert Starbright," Pie O'Sky greeted him, making a little bow.

"Pie O'Sky, I am so happy to see you."

"Are you having good Imaginings?"

"Yes, but..." Rupert wasn't sure what to say.

"What's wrong, Rupert?"

"Well, Graysland is a complicated place back here when it's before when I lived here."

Pie O'Sky smiled and shook his head as his brain tried to decipher what Rupert meant. He chuckled.

"Yes, Mr. Starbright, traveling in time can be a mind-twister!"

"And this guy Gripper—I don't know why he hates Winter Joy. Why does he want to make people all scared and stuff? I knew why Murkus did bad things. He was mad because of his baby."

"You have a big and special heart. I'm sure you can figure out why this ghost is so sad and angry. But, Rupert, if you wish to go back home right now, I can place a doorway in the back yard and you will be free to go. That choice is yours."

"But then what about Winter Joy? And Mookie? I want to find Mookie Starbright!"

"So, you wish to stay longer?"

Rupert thought about it a moment then nodded.

"Yes. I just wish I knew what to do."

"I think you do know." Pie O'Sky pointed at where his heart was and smiled.

Rupert nodded.

"Be well," Pie O'Sky said. "I am just an Imagining away if you need me, Rupert Starbright."

Rupert watched as the Great Bagoon rose beyond the trees. He waved and closed the window.

He listened at the stairwell and then at the small doorway. All was quiet. He gathered his courage and crawled back through the narrow passage. He kept his eyes shut, but he didn't feel any more spider webs. That helped him battle the fear that some of the creepy crawlies might be around him.

He bumped his nose on the door into the room with the red-glass window. He opened his eyes to peer through the crack between the door and the frame. The crate was still there. Alone. He crawled into the room, stood and approached it.

"Squeem, I'm back," he whispered.

There was no reply.

"Squeem?" He found the latch and unfastened it. He gripped the edge of the panel and pulled. The side of the crate swung out on hinges. He peered inside.

Squeem wasn't there. The big bell from the town square sat silently inside the wooden box.

"Confused?" someone asked.

Rupert spun around. Gripper, a terrible smile on his face, stared at him.

"What happened to Squeem?" Rupert demanded.

"You are quite the adversary, young Rupert. Nothing gets past those eyes of yours. Your friend is safe. For now."

Rupert felt anger bubbling in his chest, but he thought about what Pie O'Sky had just told him. *You have a big and special heart. I am sure you can figure out why this ghost is so sad and angry.*

The glass globe was burning in his pocket. He looked at Gripper and wondered what lay behind that angry face. The ghost's eyes were sadder than they were mad.

Rupert wished he could get behind them and see the world the way Gripper did.

He closed his eyes.

"What are you up to?" Gripper asked.

Rupert ignored him. He let his mind wander and Imagined his thoughts were flying across the room. They were like a bird. Like one of Folky's parakeets!

His mind entered Gripper's head and perched behind his eyes.

A flood of darkness, like a huge wave, crashed into Rupert's heart. He felt a terrible pain. Flashing images of children surrounded him. Kicking him. Mocking him. Hitting him. Laughing at him.

Ugly! Freaky face!

Rupert held his eyes shut. He needed to see more.

It was terrible as he watched Gripper, as a boy his own age, being bullied by classmates. He saw the young Gripper's face in a mirror. It was misshapen, with sunken eyes and a twisted mouth. Many pimples dotted his cheeks. He had straggly hair.

Then Rupert was in a dark place. Screaming filled his ears, and angry footsteps approached. He was under a bed. Hiding. A little ginger kitten was in his hands. Held tight. It felt warm. It was his only comfort.

Then the wind was on his face, and tears poured down as a man with a box walked off. The soft cries of a kitten came from the box his father carried away. The comfort was gone, and all again went dark.

Then he was older, and there was a fire in his heart. A face approached. A pretty face with ringlets of red hair falling around it. Warmth filled his heart.

But then there was laughter on the pretty face, and it was like a knife in the heart.

Rupert's eyes shot open. He was back behind his own eyes. A tear rolled down his cheeks. He could feel Gripper's stare.

"Stop it, Rupert."

"I'm sorry, Gripper."

"Sorry for what?"

Rupert took the globe from his pocket and held it out.

"I want you to have this. It's my Winter Joy gift to you."

Gripper stepped forward and took the globe.

"Rupert. What a generous offering," he said with a smile.

"It's okay."

Gripper's smile did a backflip and became a horrid frown. He burst into mocking laughter.

"You cannot soften me with paltry sentimental trinkets! I am not like that softy Murkus!"

Rupert felt his heart skip a beat.

"How do you know about Murkus?"

"I can let my mind fly as a bird as well. You see yourself as some great hero? Hah! You are just another big-hearted fool. Do you know what happens to big-hearted fools, my boy? Eventually, someone will take a sharp blade and pierce that big, soft heart. Then you are left with nothing!

"Listen to me. You want something? Then take it. Without thought. Without a feeling. You have a sharp mind. Use it to slice and dice those who get in your way."

Gripper stepped closer. Uncomfortably closer. His face was inches from Rupert's, and Rupert could feel and smell his breath.

"But never think you could slice me away. I can make you and your friend vanish in a flash. And then your parents and that sweet old grandmother will never ever know

139

what became of you. Even Pie O'Sky will not be able to help."

Rupert swallowed hard.

"If I were you, I would take the next door you see back to Graysland."

Rupert just stood firm.

"What did you do with Mr. Ensen?"

Gripper smiled a sour smile.

"I would get down to dinner. You do not want to miss the spectacle in the square tonight."

Gripper raised his hand, and with a swirl, he vanished into a wisp of smoke. The globe fell to the floor and shattered.

Rupert stood motionless for a moment. He wasn't sure what to do. He looked at his feet and the scattering of broken glass. He bent down to pick up the little metallic cat, but it dissolved like salt in water. The glass did as well. Rupert sighed hard and headed downstairs.

Chapter 24

Rakes on the Wing

Rupert stopped in the doorway of the dining room and froze. Jethro and Folky's mother sat around the table, as well as two of the other household staff. Ensen Starky was at the head of the small oval table. Rupert caught his eye, and for a moment, their gazes met and held. He could tell it was still Gripper in disguise. Where was the real Ensen?

"Mr. Dullz, please join us for our Winter Joy's Eve supper," said the fake Ensen.

Rupert nodded and took a seat beside Folky, who was shoving a spoonful of mashed yams into her mouth.

"Folka! Eat like a lady!" Sara scolded. She turned to Rupert. "Here you are, dear, let's fill your plate."

Rupert smiled as the wonderful aromas of lobster, broiled red snapper, baked clams, roasted mushrooms and grilled asparagus wafted to his nose. He gingerly took a piece of red snapper on his fork and sniffed.

"Don't smell your food, Rupert. Eat it!" Folky joked.

He chewed the fish, and a smile filled his eyes.

"Hey, that's good. Back home, the only fish we eat is fish-fish sandwiches. Tastes like feet and old mold."

Chuckles erupted around the table, except for Jethro who was appalled.

"I told you he's a kook, Mom," Folky said with a grin.

"Rupert, shouldn't you be spending this evening with your own family?" asked Sara.

"Uh, well…" Rupert's mind raced to come up with a decent excuse.

"I think our little friend Rupert is an orphan," the fake Ensen chimed in. "A runaway. He has been sleeping in my old study upstairs for the last few days."

Silence fell like a boulder. Folky and Rupert looked at their plates while the others stared in disbelief. Finally, her mother spoke up.

"Folga, is this true?"

Folky looked up and nodded.

"Miss Folga Tweenbort!"

"Mom, I was just trying to help. And Rupert isn't an orphan. He lives with his mom and dad and grandma."

"Tell me, Rupert. Where, exactly, do you live?" Gripper asked with a coy smirk.

Rupert looked him in the eyes. He knew Gripper was playing with his mind. Trying to upset him. Keep him on the defensive so his Imagining powers would be affected. He held the gaze and decided to tell the absolute truth.

"I'm from a town called Graysland. It's really not that far from here, but it doesn't exist yet. I came here from the future

" So, Folky is right. I live with my mom and dad and my grandma, but they're probably just kids right now or not even born yet. I want to go back, but I need a special door."

Everyone stared at him, dumbfounded. Finally, Jethro couldnt hold it in any longer. He burst into a fit of laughter. So did the rest of the table.

All but Gripper, who kept his gaze on Rupert.

"Please excuse my laughter," Jethro apologized between guffaws. "But what an imaginative young man!"

Folky's mother smiled wide then laughed.

"You're a special boy, indeed. I think you should write books! You have a wonderful mind!"

"Yes. A wonderful mind. Rupert, you may stay one more night as my guest, but tomorrow I will take you to the Gracelandville Home for Boys. We cannot have little vagabonds wandering about town. Even ones with great imaginations." Gripper let the S at the end of the word hiss like a snake.

Sara lost her smile.

"Oh. Seems like such a sad place to be on the day of The Winter Joy."

"Bah! I am tired of people using Winter Joy as an excuse for begging and sheer laziness! I have a business to run, and I will not have the added burden of another mouth to feed!"

Again silence fell on the room, but this time there was no laughter. Sara looked angry; she glared at the phony Ensen.

"Mister Starkey, you have been a generous employer, but if you prefer, I will look for housing for my daughter and I so we won't be a *burden*."

"If you must," Gripper replied. "Now let's finish our meal so we can get this bell-ringing business over with."

Rupert and Folky exchanged knowing glances as they ate in silence.

"I told you — that's not the real Mr. Starkey. It's Gripper," Rupert said as Folky checked on her birds. She closed the last cage and grabbed her jacket.

"I think you're right. Mr. Ensen would never be so mean. He loves having us live here."

"We have to make sure those bells aren't handed out. We need to sneak into that factory and destroy them."

"How?"

"I was thinking about the big vats of boiling metal. We can throw all the bells in and melt them."

"How are two kids gonna sneak into that place and not get caught?"

Rupert smiled and studied all the birds. He noticed two sturdy and very healthy parakeets tweeting away on their perch. One was bright yellow and the other a pretty sea-green. He approached their cage.

"Who are these two cool birds?"

"That's Peeper and Pooper. Pooper is the green one. They're best friends."

Rupert nodded and smiled.

"Perfect. Can I hold one?"

She nodded, and he opened the cage and put his hand in.

"What are you gonna do?"

"Come here, Pooper guy," Rupert whispered. The bird pecked at his hand but then hopped on his extended finger. He slowly pulled his hand from the cage and cradled Pooper gently in his palm.

"You take Peeper, and we'll go out to the yardback."

"You mean the back yard?"

"Whatever. And bring the gilden Gripper gave you."

Rupert knew he didn't have much time; soon, the adults would call for them to go to the town square. The bells would not be rung until the clock struck midnight. It was now nine o'clock; he hoped three hours would be enough.

Pooper's head was peeking out of Rupert's zipped jacket, and Folky held Peeper in cupped hands close to her chest. Rupert went to the red shed and removed two of the fancy rakes and laid them on the grass. His gilden was wrapped in a rag in his jacket pocket.

"You hurt my birds, and I'll whack you with a rake, Rupert Dullz!" Folky warned.

"I would never hurt birds." He took Pooper from his jacket and held him out. "Put the feed on the grass."

Folky took a handful of bird feed from her pocket and scattered it on the ground. Rupert placed Pooper down and watched as he pecked at his meal.

"Put Peeper down."

Folky did, hesitantly, and the other bird pecked at the food as well.

"Now what?" Folky asked.

Rupert sat down and closed his eyes.

"Sit and close your eyes," he said.

Folky rolled her eyes but did what he asked.

"More of this imagining stuff?"

"Focus on Peeper. I'll focus on Pooper. Just imagine that your thoughts are wrapping around her like a blanket. Think about a silver blanket that is the shiniest thing you ever saw. And the softest."

"Okay…"

"Feel it with your fingers. The moonlight is shining on it. It's like all the stars are in it."

"Hey, I can feel it!" Folky bubbled.

"Good. This isn't any normal blanket. It's a giganter blanket."

Folky chuckled. "A what?"

"A giganter blanket. It makes anything it wraps around grow real big."

"You kooky head. Okay. Hey, my giganter blanket isn't silver. It's a shiny red metal, like on the fireman's coach!"

"That's good! That means your imagination is working!"

The birds continued pecking at the seeds. A shimmer of light began glittering in the air in front of the two children.

"I can see my blanket, too. It's silver. Now, imagine the blanket is flying through the air, and it wraps around Peeper. Mine will wrap around Pooper."

"Don't suffocate my birds!"

"It won't. Can you see it?"

"Yeah!"

"Now, let the blanket wrap around the bird."

"Wow! Rupert, look!" Folky exclaimed.

Rupert opened his eyes and smiled. Two shimmering blankets of light, one red and one silver, floated through the air and descended upon the snacking parakeets.

"Now," Rupert said proudly. "Watch this…"

An adult voice interrupted the magical moment. It was Jethro.

"Okay, you two, let's get going. Mr. Ensen wants us there early."

Jethro's voice startled the birds, and they took to the sky, shimmering in a glow of red and silver.

"My birds!" Folky cried as she got up and chased after them. Thinking fast, Rupert grabbed both rakes and followed.

"Children! We have to go! No time for playing!" Jethro called after them. His voice fell on deaf ears.

Folky ran fast, searching the night sky. Flashes of red and silver zipped back and forth, but the glow seemed to be fading. She stopped in the middle of the road and stood with her head tilted back.

Rupert rushed up and looked skyward. She turned to him with tears falling down her cheeks.

"Rupert Dullz, I will never forgive you for this!"

Rupert's heart sank. *Stupid big-mouth Jethro!* he thought.

Folky turned and stomped off. Rupert didn't know what to do.

Then he saw them.

"Folky! Look!"

She turned half-heartedly and looked in the direction he was pointing. Her sad mouth burst with loud laughter. Hopping around a bend in the road came Pooper and Peeper. They were each the size of Mr. Ensen's coach! They pecked at the road, making little potholes with each peck.

Rupert smiled and handed a rake to Folky. He held his with both hands high over his head.

"Come on, Pooper! Come on, boy!"

Pooper looked at him and let out a loud squawk. He stretched his mighty wings and took to the air, soaring overhead and grabbing onto the rake with his giant talons. Up, up into the air flew Rupert!

Folky watched in awe. She followed Rupert's lead, lifting the rake with both hands high over her head.

"Come on, Peeper! Here you go, girl!"

Not wanting to be shown up by the boys, Peeper flapped her great yellow wings, snatched Folky's rake and up they rose into the dark Gracelandville sky.

From an upper window in the house, Gripper watched. He shook his head and frowned as the giant parakeets carried the two children across the skies.

"What are those runts up to?" he mumbled. He waved his arm and disappeared in a puff of mist.

Rupert's stomach was bubbling! Not since riding in Pie O'Sky's bagoon had he enjoyed the feeling of flight, but this was different. He had to hold on tight to the rake or he was done for.

The big bubble in his stomach rolled and rose into his throat, and he let out a loud burp. It was so loud Pooper turned his head and let out another squawk that sounded like a chuckle.

Rupert glanced across the sky to Peeper and discovered Folky had an ecstatic expression on her face.

"Hold on tight!" he yelled.

"Really? I was gonna hold on loosely!" Folky yelled back sarcastically.

Rupert discovered that if he twisted the rake he could make Pooper turn the way he wanted to go.

"Steer with the rake!" he shouted. "Follow me!"

He looked down and saw he was over the construction on the brand new The Curving Road.

"I could see my house from here," he yelled.

"I can see *everyone's* house from here," Folky shouted back.

He followed the rows of street lamps until he spotted the town center and then the taller buildings where the bell factory was. They would need to land on the roof.

He tugged on the rake, and after some struggle, Pooper descended a bit. As they flew across the sky, Rupert caught a glimpse of the riverside, the water glittering with moonlight.

Suddenly, Pooper's entire body shuddered and shook. Rupert's right hand slipped off the rake, and he hung by one hand. The gilden slipped from his jacket and fell down, down to the ground below.

"My bell!" he shouted.

But he was more concerned with falling himself as he tried again to grab hold of the rake. Folky gasped. Pooper shook again.

"What's wrong with him?" Rupert yelled as he managed at last to get the fingers of his right hand around the handle of the rake.

"He's gonna show you why he's called Pooper."

And, on cue, Pooper pooped. A big blob of green gook spurted and fell. Rupert watched as it dropped toward a man about to enter a horse-drawn buggy.

"Uh-oh!"

Splat!

It was a perfect shot. It landed right on the man's head and drenched his entire body. He looked skyward and shook his fist.

Folky laughed. "That's that mean old man who runs the pet shop."

"Poop-head!" Rupert joked, and they both laughed.

He could see the rooftop they needed to land on. He yanked on the rake to get Pooper to bank left then tugged to get him to descend. Folky did the same.

"Land on that building with the big chimney," he said.

"Hey! What are those?"

A flock of flaming birds was heading right at them! They zoomed by like meteors. The heat was intense, and the parakeets squawked and panicked. Peeper and Pooper veered off at full speed. Rupert gripped the rake handle tight and could only hope their birds did the same. Glancing behind, he could see the mysterious fiery critters arching around for another attack.

"They're coming back!"

"Imagine something, Rupert!" Folky pleaded.

He took a deep breath and was about to close his eyes when he looked down and gasped. They were over the river and heading towards the vast sea beyond!

Chapter 25

In His Grip

Rupert hadn't expected this, and his arms were growing tired. He looked at Folky, and she looked as scared as he felt.

"Rupert! Look out!" she screamed.

The flaming birds were all around him.

Pooper squawked and flapped his wings wildly, as if trying to shoo off the creatures.

"Please, calm down, Pooper." Rupert turned to Folky and shouted. "We have to turn around. Get to the roof!"

The bird wasn't listening, though, and Peeper was getting scared as well as some of the fiery critters came her way. Rupert's mind raced. He looked down at the river, and it seemed like a lifetime ago he had been on board the deck as the *Tall Tale* was engulfed in flames.

Of course! he thought. *Fire hates water!*

He yanked on the rake, hoping Pooper would fly down towards the river. Instead, he just went on flapping crazily and flying in circles, trying to avoid the fire birds. Peeper was doing the same thing.

"Hurry, Rupert!" Folky yelled as Peeper began to fly in a spiraling path higher and higher.

Then Rupert saw it. A cloud. A single dark cloud was forming over their heads. It was unfolding like a big, comfy blanket.

A flaming bird struck Pooper on his tush, and he screeched. Rupert smelled burning feathers.

"Hang in there, Pooper!"

Another fiery bird zipped by Rupert's head; he felt the heat. But there was something else. A sudden black feeling of fear was slipping into his mind.

It wasn't the normal fear of being high over the world hanging on a rake in the grip of a giant parakeet. That was a normal fear that any kid in their right mind would be feeling if they were in Rupert's or Folky's shoes.

No. This was different. It was a fear that made no sense. It was like a stomach ache in his mind. It was like the Darkledroons.

Rupert had enough problems. He had to clear his head and let his Imaginings work.

At that moment, a flash of light filled the night.

"Yes!" He grinned. Where there's lightning, there's *rain!*

A clap of thunder opened the floodgates. A heavy downpour began falling from the lone cloud over their heads. One by one, the fire birds fizzled out into little puffs of harmless steam.

Rupert had not Imagined any of it—he hadn't been able to focus his thoughts. Somehow, a cloud had appeared and saved the day. He looked over at Folky, and she winked.

"Great Imaginings, Folky!" he shouted, proud of her.

The parakeets had grown calmer and started chirping happily. They seemed to be enjoying the shower.

Rupert tugged on the rake, and Pooper began to descend. Folky followed. The rain stopped as quickly as it had started, and the cloud dissolved away. The two giant parakeets soared back over town as Rupert scanned for the rooftop.

"The tall one! Make her land there!" he ordered.

Pooper cruised over the tallest rooftop, and Rupert decided to just let go of the rake and drop the ten feet or so. He stumbled and ended up on on his bottom but was very relieved to be on solid ground again. He stood up and waved wildly at Peeper and Folky, who were quickly approaching, waited for them to get close.

"Jump!" he shouted as the giant bird cruised overhead.

Folky let go of the rake and landed on her feet. She lifted her arms in the air victoriously. The two giant birds flew a few circles then perched on the raised edge of the roof. They shrank back to their normal size. Folky raced over and gently picked them up and placed them in her her jacket.

"That was nuts," Rupert said, catching his breath.

"That was great!" Folky said, super-excited. "Where did those fire birds come from?"

"I'm pretty sure I know."

"Gripper?" Folky guessed.

Rupert nodded.

"Why is he so mean?"

"I think I know why. Every since he was a kid, people made fun of him. He had no friends. Even this girl that he liked hurt him bad. He's mad at the world."

"That's sad. But he still shouldn't try to knock a kid off a giant bird over the river!" Folky said. Her voice cracked with anger.

"I know," Rupert agreed. "Mr. Ensen said he got gold-hungry. It's all he cares about. Maybe because the gold can't hurt him the way people did?" He spotted the entrance to the building and headed towards it. "Come on."

The roof entrance opened on a dark staircase, and Rupert and Folky carefully climbed down each creaky step, trying to make as little noise as possible. At the bottom was another door. Rupert put his ear against it.

"It's quiet," he whispered.

He opened the door and peered into another stairwell, lit only by a single yellow lightbulb. The air smelled of burning metal and old dust. They crept onto the landing.

"We have to go all the way down to the first floor. That's where the bell factory is," whispered Rupert. "Wish we had more light."

"You mean like this?"

Folky pulled a pen-sized object from her pocket and held it out.

"Light!" she commanded. A beam of bright light shot from it.

"A flashlamp! I didn't think they were invented yet back now!" Rupert said with excitement.

"There's only one like it. Mr. Ensen invented it. He never showed it to anyone else. Said people weren't ready to see it."

"Can I see it?"

"Only if you promise to give it back."

"I will."

She handed it to him, and he studied the silver device. There were no switches on it like the big, heavy flashlamp his father had. It didn't have a cap you could unscrew if you needed to put batteries in. In fact, he couldn't even see a lightbulb! The white light seemed to just pour out of one end like water from a faucet.

Rupert raised his eyebrows, and the smile came back onto his face.

"Mr. Ensen didn't invent this. Mr. Ensen Imagined it!"

He led the way down to the next landing, where another door waited. Rupert took hold of the doorknob and turned. It came loose. Only it wasn't a doorknob. It was a bell! He dropped it like a hot coal.

Ringing echoed around them.

"Oh, no," Rupert muttered. "A trap."

Folky tapped him on the shoulder, and he turned to see her staring up to the top of staircase. She looked sick. Three giant spiders began to slowly climb down the steps with their hairy legs.

Rupert stood frozen. They crawled closer, hissing like snakes.

"Rupert, we have to go!"

The spiders came closer, but Rupert was too frozen with fear to move an inch. Folky shook him, trying to snap him back.

"Rupert! Imagine something!"

He swallowed hard as the spiders inched closer.

Folky had enough of the waiting and shoved Rupert aside. She pushed on the door.

"It's locked," she said. "Try to Imagine something."

Rupert closed his eyes and tried very hard to clear his mind of the terrors that were creeping their way. His thoughts were filled with cobwebs.

He battled the darkness in his head, but there was only a flicker of light like a faraway candle. He focused on it.

"Ruuuuppppeeeeert!" wailed a ghostly voice from far off. Rupert knew that voice almost better than his own. His eyes popped open.

"Squeem? Where are you?" he shouted. Folky was confused.

"I am in trouble! The houuussssse is on ffffiirrrrrre!"

"Who is that?" Folky asked.

"My best friend Squeem," Rupert said. "Squeem, what house are you in?"

"The one on Old Homes Rrrrroad. Back wherrrrre we livvvve!"

"But you were just in that box in the house back now!" Rupert protested.

"Gripper sent me baaaack! Into the firrre!"

The spiders were no more that ten feet away. Rupert again closed his eyes to try and grab hold of his Imagining powers.

Folky gasped.

"Look, Rupert!"

Rupert opened his eyes and gasped as well. At the top of the stairs appeared a ghostly image of flames. Standing in the middle of the inferno was Squeem.

"Squeem!"

"Help me!" Squeem shouted.

"I have to do something! Help me imagine!" Rupert pleaded with Folky.

"You need to imagine the door back to our time, Rupert Starbright!" Squeem said, his voice changing and growing deeper.

Rupert's frowned and looked at Folky.

"Squeem's not really in danger! That's not real. None of this is! This is all tricks of Gripper! Just like the fire birds!"

"How can you be so sure?"

"Squeem would never call me Rupert Starbight. He thinks it's the dumbest name!"

Folky kicked at one of the spiders that had crept too close for comfort. Her foot went right through it!

"Hey! You're right! That spider is just a mirage!"

"A what?" Rupert asked.

"A trick. Like seeing water on a dry road on a hot day. Don't you learn anything in school?"

The world around them shimmied and shook. A terrible laugh echoed up and down the stairwell.

"You had your chance, Rupert Starbright!" thundered the wicked voice of Gripper. "Your friend may not be in danger yet, but he will be unless you stay out of my affairs. Neither he nor another friend of yours will ever see the light of day again!"

"He must have Mr. Ensen, too!" Folky guessed.

"Where are they?" Rupert demanded.

"I will release them once you have passed through the door back to your own time, where you will not pester me or meddle in my business."

"You're afraid of Rupert!" Folky shouted.

Her laughter bounded around the narrow space.

"You are!" she insisted. "Gripper is a big old chicken afraid of a kid!" Folky stuck her tongue out and laughed.

The world shook again, and Rupert and Folky almost fell over. There was the sound of a lock mechanism clicking, and the door swung open. Folky grabbed his hand.

"Come on!"

"Wait! Might be a trap," Rupert warned.

He peered through the doorway and saw it opened into a large warehouse filled with fanciful coaches. The light was dim and yellow from rows of lightbulbs that hung bare from the ceiling. At the far end of the room was a metal cage with an elevator platform. He knew what to do.

"Let's go."

They jogged across the room, keeping an eye on the coaches to be sure no one was waiting to pounce.

"The bells are on the first floor. We can take this elevator."

"Cool!" Folky said excitedly. "I've never been on one before." She peeked into her jacket and checked on Peeper and Pooper. "Hey, guys, ready for an elevator ride?"

Peeps and tweets sang out.

Rupert opened the gate and stepped onto the open platform that was large enough to hold two coaches. Folky came aboard, and he closed the gate then scanned the control panel and found the DOWN button. He pressed it.

The elevator descended past another large warehouse that was filled with row after row of large wooden crates. Down they went past another floor that was one big, empty space, except for a large cage in the center. Two people sat on the floor of in the cage—a boy and a man.

Rupert hit the STOP button, and the pulley system squealed to a stop. The two people got up and stared at the elevator. It was Squeem and Ensen Starkey.

Chapter 26

Not Even a Mouse

"Rupert!" Squeem shouted. "Get us out of here!"

"It's Mr. Ensen and some boy," Folky said excitedly.

"This is probably another trap." Rupert scanned the room.

"Rupert, you have to get us out of here! There's some horrible—"

Before Squeem could finish his sentence, there came a nerve shattering roar.

"…monster," Squeem finished.

Something huge moved at the far end of the room and began to come toward them. As it moved through the pools of light from the bulbs overhead, Rupert saw it had two heads—one bright blue and the other a fiery red. The body was like a tyrannosaurus's, but its tail was lined with deadly spikes. From the nostrils of the blue head came flashes and sparks of electricity, and smoky fire spouted from the red head.

"What is *that*?" Folky whispered.

"More mirages," Rupert said, never taking his eyes off the creature.

"Mirage or not, that thing is scary!" Folky said.

The creature let loose a blast of lightning and fire. Rupert's eyes bugged, and he slammed his fist on the DOWN button.

"Rupert, you have to save us!" Squeem cried out.

"Take care, you two mirages!" Rupert shouted back.

Fire washed into the elevator as it lowered. Rupert and Folky dropped the floor, and they could feel the heat and sizzle. The roar of the beast faded as they traveled down, down and down until they reached the bottom floor.

Rupert opened the gate and stepped off the platform. They were in a wide hallway. He sniffed the air. It had a familiar odor.

"That's the stink of the liquid metal. The bell factory is this way."

He rushed down the hall until it came to a T. He could smell fresh air. He followed his nose until he came to another hall that ended in the familiar doors that led to Shadow Lane. Opposite it was the door to the bell factory and its pulsing sound of machinery inside.

He looked at Folky, pressed his finger to his lips and tiptoed to the factory door.

He peeked in. There were three workers, the same three who had delivered the wooden crate to Mr. Ensen's house.

"We need a plan to get them out of the room," he whispered. "Think your birds could distract them?"

"No way!" Folky said, too loudly. Rupert shushed her with a firm finger to his lips.

"Maybe one of us could run in there and get chased. Then the other could go in and take care of the bells," he suggested.

"For a kid with such a great imagination, those are dumb ideas," Folky said.

Rupert nodded. He needed to just walk in and ask them to leave. Simple as that. Maybe he could be really convincing and tell them there was a fire and they had to leave. Or that the moon was falling and was going to crush the building.

Nah. He needed to speak with authority. He needed to make them scared as if it were Gripper yelling orders at them.

Gripper!

"Hey," Rupert whispered. "If Gripper can make himself look like Mr. Starkey then maybe I can make myself look like Gripper."

"You're too short, kook head!"

"I can Imagine I'm taller. We made your birds bigger."

"Well, please hurry. This place is creepy." Folky scanned the hallway.

Rupert closed his eyes and saw Gripper in his mind. He saw his face and its cold eyes. He saw the long, skinny body and creepy cloak. Gripper's laughter tickled his brain. It grew louder and louder.

There was a scream. Rupert opened his eyes, and Folky was staring up at him with horror in her eyes.

She was looking *up* at him.

"What's wrong?" His voice sounded different. It felt different in his throat.

Folky could barely get the words out.

"You're Gripper."

"Cool!" Rupert said. He looked down at his body and chuckled. "I feel so weird being tall!"

"Rupert, please get this over with. You're making me sick." She was pressing both hands to her stomach.

Rupert smiled and entered the bell factory room. The men were placing dozens of silver bells on a table. The vat of gold bubbled, and the little man was placing a piece of the golden armor from the skeletons into the hot metal. A couple of bells that had been coated in the terrible gold sat on another table. Dozens of silver bells awaited their coats of the nightmare-making gold.

"Stop at once!" Rupert shouted, his voice booming like Gripper's.

All heads turned his way. A look of terror filled their eyes.

"Sir, what an unexpected honor!" said the head workman.

"I want you all to stop this work at once! Leave! Go home and be with your families!"

The men's expressions went from fear to complete confusion. The little man stepped forward and bowed.

"That is very kind, good sir. But what about the rest of the bells. They will need time to dry once they have been dipped. Shouldn't we finish the job at hand?"

"Yes, you should!"

It wasn't Rupert. The real Gripper stepped into the room, dragging Folky by the arm. All eyes bounced between the two tall, cloaked men. No one knew what to say.

"It would appear that a child is playing a prank on you. I order you all to continue your work and finish the bells!"

"This is a fake Gripper!" Rupert shouted. "Do not listen to him!"

The real Gripper laughed.

"He's right! This fake Gripper is scared of a kid!" Folky said.

"You young fools have over-stepped your bounds for the last time!" Gripper snarled.

He raised his arms, and a flash of green light swirled around him and engulfed Rupert. Rupert shrank, and his

Gripper disguise melted away. Soon, he was back to being eleven year old Rupert, all four feet, ten inches of him.

The workers laughed.

"Now finish the bells!" Gripper ordered.

The workers turned back to their task.

Rupert stood firm.

"Gripper is just a bully because he was made fun of as a kid!"

"Yeah, he's really just a big chicken!" Folky added. "He knows how powerful Rupert is, and he's afraid of him!"

"Enough of your mouths, little worms!" Gripper said. "Be off! Or I will see to it you will never see the light of day again!"

"Ha!" Folky laughed. "Rupert, turn him into a worm!"

All eyes were on Rupert as he nodded, closed his eyes and raised his arms.

Gripper flinched. It was just for a second, but that was enough. The workers were watching with raised eyebrows.

"Fools!" Gripper said.

"See! You're scared of Rupert! You're nothing but a big chicken! All bullies are!"

Folky began to laugh. Rupert watched as one of the workers bit his lip then burst into laughter as well.

Rupert raised his arms overhead and made a monster face.

Gripper flinched again.

"Big chicken face!" Folky said.

The workmen, too, began to laugh.

Gripper's face turned burning red. He looked at each person laughing at him.

Rupert closed his eyes and let his Imaginings fly into Gripper's mind. He saw his thoughts, and even worse, he felt what the old, mean ghost was feeling.

Everything slowed down as the mocking guffaws hit him like arrows. His mind raced, and horrible memories filled his head.

Gripper's anger exploded, and he screamed a terrible scream. He pushed Folky towards Rupert, and a flare of light burst from his mouth. A giant bubble encased Rupert and Folky in a glass prison.

All was silent for a moment.

"What are we gonna do?" Folky said, looking scared again. "We're trapped."

"I have an idea," Rupert said confidently.

Gripper crept closer to the bubble and smiled fiendishly at Rupert.

"Who is laughing now?" he hissed.

Rupert smiled. Wide. He held something behind his back. He looked Gripper in the eyes.

"Don't matter," Rupert said. "You have that little vat of gold, but what I have makes that look like a pot of mud."

"What foolishness are you talking?"

"Nothing. Not your business. Just something I imagined."

"What? Another foolish snow globe?"

"No. Something you never dreamed of but you've wanted all your life," Rupert teased.

"As if you would know what a man like me wants."

"I do. You love gold. What I have is the answer to your dreams."

Rupert held out the object he had behind his back. It was a rod, glistening with golden light.

The workers' eyes widened at the sight.

"What is that?" Gripper asked trying to hide his interest.

"A gold tapper-wapper," Rupert said.

"What nonsense. Stupid name!" Gripper spat.

"Really? Wouldn't you love to have an object that can turn anything it touches into solid gold?" Rupert asked.

"You mean fool's gold!" Gripper said with an awkward laugh.

"No, I mean real gold. Watch."

Rupert tapped the device on Folky's shoulder, and she turned into a golden statue. The workers gasped.

Gripper all but drooled.

"Clever, my boy. Very clever. Nice trick. I have seen magicians pull off more convincing tricks."

"Trick? No. This is real. It works. And you know it." Rupert never moved his gaze from Gripper. "You want this so bad you can taste it."

Gripper turned in a rage.

"Give me that!"

"Nope. It's mine!" Rupert stuck out his tongue. "I Imagined it, and only I can Imagine such a thing. You could never!"

"I said I want it!!"

The rage in his voice startled Rupert but also made him feel sad. He shook his head and held it out.

"If this means so much to you then you can have it. *If* you let us out and let us go back home."

"I don't negotiate with half-pint know-it-alls!"

"If you want this and all the gold you can ever dream of then, that's the deal. Or I'll just Imagine it away!"

"No! Don't do that!"

"Do we have a deal?" Rupert asked.

"Yes. Yes, you can leave. And we can place your golden friend in the town square like a statue!"

Rupert nodded and held out the golden tapper-wapper rod. Gripper waved his hand, and the glass prison dissolved away. He snatched the rod from Rupert's hand and lifted it high with a crazed expression on his face.

There was a *ting-tingle* sound. Gripper gasped. He now realized the trick—what he held in his hand was a golden bell. Rupert's Imaginings had simply disguised it. In a flash, Gripper was transformed into a small, white mouse. A powerless, weak, meek mouse that sat frozen in fear.

Rupert looked at Folky, whose golden disguise faded away. She glared at him.

"Rupert, I should slug you for that!" she said, looking around. "Hey, where did Gripper go?"

Rupert gestured at the mouse then knelt down and took the little critter into his hand.

"This was his greatest fear. To be powerless and small." He looked sadly at the mouse. "You were always empty inside. You thought that gold would fill the hole in your heart. People were mean to you, and you thought bullying was the answer. Now you're what you were always afraid you would be. A helpless little creature."

"I feel bad for him," Folky said softly.

"Me, too."

The mouse squeaked pitifully. The workers gathered around and stared at it.

"We should crush that bugger with a shovel!" cried one.

"Or feed him to the butcher's cat!" said another.

"No, I will eat him whole!" laughed the little man.

"*No!* We won't hurt him," Rupert told them.

"He was a monster! He made us do his terrible deeds" the little man said.

"I know. But he was a ghost. Not even a man. A ghost who came back to find a way to be happy and just found more sad stuff. He never really knew that gold and money can't make you happy if you hate everybody."

Folky smiled and put her hand on Rupert's shoulder.

"You're a pretty smart kid."

Rupert smiled.

"What are we gonna do with him? He's kinda cute this way," Folky continued. The birds in her jacket tweeted.

165

"I'm not sure. We need to find out what he did with Squeem and Mr. Ensen."

The mouse began squeaking and squealing wildly.

"Maybe he's trying to tell us something?" Folky suggested.

"Maybe I need to Imagine him back to a ghost man so he can tell us."

The workers backed off.

"No! He'll kill us all!" the little man said.

"I'm leaving this awful place!" said the middle-sized man and raced out. The other two followed.

"First, we have to melt all the bells," Rupert said. "Make sure you don't ring any."

"Rupert." Folky had a worried look on her face. "What about the bell you dropped from the sky?"

"One thing at a time, Grandma. I mean, Folky," Rupert quickly corrected. He blushed, and she mouthed the word *kookadoo* to herself.

They dropped the silver bells into the bubbling vat and watched as they melted and dissolved into little pools of silver that vanished into the gold. The mouse began to squeak and squeal again, fidgeting wildly until he managed to free himself from Rupert's grasp.

Gripper the mouse raced out of the room. Rupert and Folky followed.

Chapter 27

The Story Told

"Where is he?" Folky shouted.

"There!"

The mouse raced down the long hallway then turned right onto the wide part of the corridor. He raced to the end and to Rupert's surprise, hopped on the elevator platform and just sat there. Waiting.

"Look. He's waiting for us," Rupert said.

"Maybe he wants us to take him upstairs."

Rupert slowly approached the elevator with Folky behind him.

"It's okay, mouse. We won't hurt you," he said softly.

He stepped onto the platform, but the mouse just stood silently, eyeing them both with a twitchy nose. Folky joined them.

"Nowhere to go but up," Rupert said as he closed the gate and pushed the red button marked UP.

Up they went. They passed floor after floor, until they reached the empty room with the cage. They were prepared to duck in case the monster was waiting to blast them, and Rupert kept his fingers hovering over the DOWN button. Just in case.

When they stepped into the room, the mouse ran to the cage, its little nose twitching and sniffing.

"Rupert! Get us out of here!" the boy who looked like Squeem shouted.

"Think it's a trap?" Folky asked.

"It has to be," Rupert said.

"It's not a trap, dumbhead! It's me, Squeem!"

"He is telling the truth, Rupert," Ensen insisted.

"What about that monster?" Rupert asked, trying to decide if they *were* telling the truth.

"He vanished into the shadows. Please, let us out before he shows up again!" Squeem pleaded.

Gripper the mouse seemed to be trying to convince Rupert as well with his high-pitched squeaks.

Rupert took a few cautious steps toward the cage, and for the first time noticed it was shimmering with a strange blue-black light that trickled along the bars like jelly.

"Prove you're really Squeem," he demanded.

"How?" Squeem asked.

"Tell me something only we know."

Squeem nodded and paced as he wracked his brain. He then smiled and looked at Rupert.

"When we were in first grade, I dared you to eat that stubby-tree leaf, and you did, but it turned out to really be a bluefrog-oak leaf."

"And my face got all covered with warts for three days, " Rupert said with a blush.

"And you had to put that cream on them that smelled just like old cheese."

Folky made a funny face, wrinkling her nose as if she could smell it.

"Yuk!"

"Okay, I guess it's really you."

Ensen spoke up. "Rupert, we need you to use your Imaginings to get us out of here before Gripper returns."

"Gripper *did* return," Rupert told him, gesturing at the mouse.

"Rupert Imagined him into a mouse!" Folky said with pride.

"Amazing!" Ensen gasped. "Your Imagining abilities are even greater than..."

"Than yours, Mr. Starkey?" Rupert said with a smile.

The Gripper mouse began squealing and squeaking.

"The monster's back!" Folky shouted, pointing across the room.

Sure enough, the two-headed beast had stepped from a dark corner. It threw back its heads and let out a roar that was mixed with spurts of fire and electricity.

"Can you Imagine something, Rupert?" Folky asked, her eyes never leaving the creature.

"Of course he can," Ensen said confidently.

"Kill it!" Squeem shouted.

"I think he can Imagine something better than that. Am I right, Rupert?" Ensen asked with a smile. "I think the quaint words of wisdom of your father may help."

Rupert thought for a moment and smiled at him.

"If you planted the tree, then you must rake the leaves."

Rupert knelt down closer to the mouse then took it into his hands.

"You planted this tree, Gripper, so you have to rake the leaves."

"What's that suppose to mean," Squeem asked.

"Gripper created the monster. He has to stop it," Rupert explained then turned back to the mouse. "You can help make up for the bad you did if you can use your Imaginings now. Me and you together."

169

He bravely stepped closer to the monster, holding the mouse out before him in his cupped hands. The mouse squeaked, and the monster stopped and looked at it curiously.

"Come on, buddy! Let's see what you have!" Rupert challenged.

The mouse squeaked again, and the monster puffed a little fire from its right head and grunted. Behind them, Folky's birds squawked nervously, and Rupert could hear the rustle as they flapped their wings inside her jacket. She spoke to them softly to calm them.

Rupert took another bold step closer.

"What's wrong? Afraid of a little mouse?" He laughed.

Rupert dashed a few steps towards the creature, and it backed away keeping its glowing eyes on Rupert. Gripper squeaked louder, and the monster replied with a whining grunt.

"You're afraid of this mouse because this mouse is your master! This little mouse Imagined you!" Rupert said, laughing more.

Folky's birds were chirping up a storm.

Rupert was just a few feet from the massive legs of the beast. He could feel the heat from the flames and smell the sharp aroma of electricity burning the air around them. He put one hand on his hip and used the other to hold Gripper the mouse up before him. The monster lowered its heads to get a closer look.

"You can't blast me because you might blast Gripper. And if Gripper disappears, so will you. Right, buddy?" Rupert asked.

The monster stared back with rather stupid expressions on its faces. It threw its heads back and let out a pathetic cry, sending bursts of fire and electricity at the ceiling.

Folky's birds had had enough. They escaped from her jacket and began flying in crazed circles around the room. The creature's attention turned to the birds, and its two foreheads wrinkled.

"They're just friendly birds!" Rupert insisted.

Gripper squealed. The birds landed on the floor and squawked at the monster angrily. It seemed to smile a devilish smirk and aimed its deadly mouths.

Folky screamed and raced to her birds. Gripper the mouse leapt off Rupert's hand and did the same.

It all seemed to happen in slow motion. Folky dived for her birds as blasts of fire and lightning slammed the floor. A cloud of scorched dust flew up and covered Folky.

Gripper the mouse rushed to the monster's foot and clamped its little teeth down on one giant toe. The creature roared and sent out another blast of fire and electricity.

Poor little Gripper the mouse vanished, and the monster, realizing its mistake too late, dissolved away into nothingness. The Imaginer and the Imagined were both gone.

Rupert rushed to Folky, who lay on the floor motionless. She was covered in ash and dust.

"Folky! You okay?"

"Yeah. Is that thing done trying to cook my birds?" she mumbled.

Rupert smiled.

"Yes. He's gone. And so is Gripper." There was a touch of sadness in his voice.

Folky rolled over, and Rupert burst into laughter. Her face was coated in gray ash. She stood up, the two birds safely in hand.

"What's so funny? My birds almost got toasted!"

"Are you okay?" he said, trying not to laugh. "You look pretty silly."

She coughed and pushed him playfully.

"Hey! What about us?" Squeem yelled from the cage.

Rupert had almost forgotten about his friend and Mr. Starkey. He rushed to the cage and searched for the door. There wasn't one.

"I wonder why the cage didn't vanish when Gripper did? He imagined this," he wondered.

"No, he didn't," Squeem said. "Mr. Ensen did. It's a fire-and-electricity-proof cage."

"I imagined it to keep us safe from that thing," Ensen explained.

Rupert smiled and stepped closer, looking him in the eyes,

"You're Mookie Starbright, aren't you?"

Ensen nodded and gave Rupert a knowing wink of his eye.

"Can you make the cage disappear so we can get out?" Squeem asked him, sounding annoyed.

"I think Rupert can get us out. He just needs to use the key around his neck," Ensen said.

Rupert grasped at the chain around his neck and felt the object hanging from it.

"My fish key!" he said with delight.

"Just ask it to free us," Ensen told him.

Rupert nodded but lost his smile.

"Just one question," he said. "Who was Gripper?"

Ensen took a deep breath and exhaled hard.

"Bolton Gripper was the first man to invest in my company. He was stubborn and would stop at nothing to get what he wanted. His greed made him sick. He told me one day he was dying. He promised he would make me a very rich man if I could imagine he would live longer.

"I did, but life and death are very complicated things, so I was only able to make him a ghost, trapped between life and *unlife*. Then he convinced me to imagine that he would have Imagining. I never realized how greedy for power he was until it was too late."

"That's sad," Folky said.

"Yes, Folky. But Rupert was wise. He knew if Gripper faced his fears he would open his heart. Gripper feared being powerless. Like a little mouse. But that little mouse found his courage, and he roared!"

"He did. He saved my birds," Folky said, coughing more.

"He saved us all," Rupert added. "Okay, fishkey, free my friends from this cage."

In a flourish of colorful, glowing glitter, the fishkey flew through the air and formed a circle of light around the cage, which quickly melted away like ice too close to the sun. The key returned to the chain around Rupert's neck.

"Shall we go to the town square for a little Winter Joy celebration?" Ensen asked.

"Yes!" Folky said then coughed some more.

"What about the big bell? It's in a box in that room at the top of your house."

Ensen grew serious and nodded.

"All will be fine. Let's go to the square. We'll get your mom, Folga. She must be worried sick. I think we have all earned a happy evening.

Folky and Squeem hurried toward the elevator, but Rupert stayed back for a private word with Ensen.

"Mr. Starkey," he said in a low voice, "how did you find out you have Imagining?"

Ensen looked to him and smiled fondly as memories filled his mind.

"My thoughts were always filled with adventures and stories. I would lie awake at night under the covers of my bed and imagine I was traveling to far-off places and meeting all sorts of exciting people. Then, one day when I was pulling up old, boring weeds in my backyard, a colorful man descended from the sky in a great balloon. Only he called it a *bagoon*."

"Pie O'Sky!" Rupert guessed happily.

Ensen nodded. "He made me realize that I had — that we all have — that great magic inside us all."

"So how come you started making rakes and all kinds of other boring stuff?"

Ensen chuckled.

"I got distracted by money. Not money I got because I was making and selling things but money for the sake of having even more money. *That*, Rupert, was *really* boring."

"So, what are you gonna do now?"

"What I've wanted to do for years. I'm going to find a little house in a magical little clump of trees by a stream and use my Imagining to write as many just-because stories as I can."

"That's definitely not boring, Mr. Starkey!"

"Call me Mookie, Rupert Starbright."

They both smiled and went to join Folky and Squeem.

Chapter 28

The Last Bell

The town square was bustling, lights glittered, and a chilly breeze danced through the streets like an excited child. There was a hum of conversation and looks of confusion. Folky spotted her mother and Jethro and raced to them.

"Folky! Where have you been?" Sara asked, grabbing her chin sternly.

"Mom, you'll never believe it. You should have seen what happened." Her excitement was interrupted by a fit of coughing. "…a mouse and then this giant monster…"

"Are you getting sick?" Sara felt Folky's forehead for fever.

"I'm fine. Oh, this is Rupert's friend Squeem."

Squeem, who had followed her over, nodded shyly.

"Hello, Squeem. Where have you two delinquents been?" Sara asked sternly.

"Three delinquents," Ensen said, mussing Squeem's hair. "Actually, it was my fault, Sara. They were helping me with a project. I should have made sure you knew."

175

"Yes, Mr. Starkey you most certainly should have."

"You should have seen Rupert, Mom! He turned that old Gripper into a mouse—"

"Folga, we are here to celebrate Winter Joy and not go on with your tall tales. Bad enough everyone's groaning and moaning about Winter Joy being a waste without the big bell."

"I think they're silly," Folky said.

Her mother smiled.

"I agree. It's not about bells and lights. It's about the joy of helping others."

Sara gave Ensen a sharp glance.

"You are so right, Sara. That is the real spirit of Winter Joy, not the decorations."

She frowned.

"So, why, may I ask, did you take the bell from the square and put it in your home?"

Ensen shook his head.

"That was not my decision, and I promise it will be returned."

"It was that mean old Gripper that took the bell, Mom, but we all stopped him."

"Folka is quite a special young lady. And her friend Rupert is special as well. Right, Squeem?"

"Yes!" Squeem said with pride.

"So, what happens now?" Rupert asked.

Jethro cleared his throat and puffed out his chest.

"With or without the Gildengroat, the great Cat Aranthal will come, " Jethro said. "Look."

He pointed to the sky.

Peeking out through breaks in the thick layer of clouds were two bright stars, like two eyes looking down at the world.

"The Winter Cat is here."

Rupert and Squeem looked up and smiled.

"When does everyone ring the bells?" Rupert wanted to know.

"Speaking of which," Sara asked. "What happened to your special bells Mr. Ensen gave you?"

Before Rupert or Folky could answer, Ensen did.

"Those bells were...faulty. We made sure the entire batch was destroyed."

"The entire batch but that one!" Rupert pointed across the square at a boy about his own age who held in his hand a golden bell.

Folky gasped.

"That must be the one you dropped!" she whispered to Rupert.

He nodded and dashed across the square to face the boy.

"Hey, kid!" He said in as friendly a voice as he could muster.

"Yeah?" the boy replied with a sneer.

"That bell you have. You found it near that old red-and-green barn?"

"Maybe? Why? What do you care?"

"It's no good. Whole mess o' bells, the gold ones — no good. Won't ring right, and you'll get the Cat all mad, and you won't get any Winter Joy gifts."

The boy studied Rupert curiously then held the bell up in front of his eyes.

"Nothing wrong with it. You're just trying to get me to ring it early. Bad luck for early ringers. No way! I'm waiting for that big ol' clock to hit midnight. Then I'm gonna ring this bell, and you'll see. I'll wake up tomorrow and have way more gifts from the Cat then you. You don't even have a bell!"

Rupert glanced across the square at the large and fanciful clock that sat on top of the Gracelandville Bank building. Less than a minute was left until midnight.

177

He had to think fast. If this pain-in-the-neck kid rang the bell than whatever he feared most would appear. What if this kid's fear was a giant dragon or rains of fire? Then the entire town would run home scared and never want to celebrate Winter Joy again!

What if he's afraid of something silly? Something that everyone else would think was great? What if he's afraid of pink snowflakes or silver butterflies? What if gumdrops scare him... or kittens?

There were thirty seconds left.

"Hey, kid," Rupert asked. "What are you scared of?"

"Me? Nothing! I ain't a'scared o' nuthin!"

"What about snowflakes or kittens?"

"You're a kook. Leave me alone. I have to get ready to ring my bell!"

Rupert exhaled hard. He glanced at the clock. Ten seconds!

There was a sudden excitement in the crowd.

"Let the countdown begin!" Jethro cried.

Everyone began to call out the numbers in unison.

"Ten!"

Rupert's mind raced.

"Nine!"

What to do?

"Eight!"

He had a thought. It was simple.

"Seven!"

He gazed at the bell in the boy's hand.

"Six!" cried the crowd,

He took a step closer.

"five!"

He got ready.

"Four!"

The boy slowly lift the bell higher.

"Three!"

Rupert pounced.

"Two!"

He grabbed the bowl of the bell and yanked on it. The boy turned and angrily pulled it back by the handle.

"Let go!" Rupert shouted.

"No!" the boy shouted back.

"*One!*"

Rupert yanked on the bell harder, and it slipped from both of their grips. It flew skyward as if in slow motion, and Rupert watched as it seemed to hang in the air for a moment then fall. Both he and the other boy reached for it, but Rupert was faster. He caught it by the handle.

The little gold bell rang. Rupert gasped and he felt his heart sink into his stomach.

"*Happy Winter Joy!*" cried the crowd.

"Dumbhead! I'm telling my mother!" the boy cried, rushing off.

Rupert stared at the bell in his hands. All around him people were hugging and wishing each other a good holiday.

What had he done? He tried to think which one of his fears was about to come true? Spiders? He looked around and didn't see a single hairy eight-legged critter.

Drowning? Not a drop of water to be seen.

Then he heard a familiar sound, and it echoed in his mind. He turned to see Folky coughing.

His greatest fear was that he would never find a *real* cure for his grandmother's coffus.

"Rupert!" Folky shouted, running over to join him. "Happy Winter Joy!"

Rupert was holding the golden bell by the handle as if he were holding a dead rat by the tail. Folky noticed it, and her smile vanished. Squeem had followed her.

"Did you ring it?" she asked.

Rupert nodded, his head down, and stared at his feet. He suddenly looked up and forced a smile.

"But nothing happened! Dumb old Gripper. Couldn't even get that right!"

Folky gave him a big hug.

"Happy Winter Joy, Rupert Starbright!"

"Happy Winter Joy, Grandma—I mean, Folky."

The crowd began to head home to continue the celebration. There were mumbles about the missing bell and how *Winter Joy just isn't how it used to be*. Jethro headed off to get the coach.

Ensen stepped up to Rupert and put a hand on his shoulder; he smiled as he looked across the square.

"I think our friend has visited." He pointed past the buildings toward a dirt road where there was a clump of trees. Next to it was a red door. A door in a frame.

Rupert's smile was mixed with a little sadness. He knew it was time for him to head home. He glanced skyward and smiled. Pie O'Sky's bagoon drifted with the eyes of Aranthal twinkling behind it.

"What are you looking at?" Folky asked.

"That." Rupert pointed to the door. "Time I go home."

"Oh." She seemed saddened by the news.

"Don't worry. I have a feeling we'll run into each other again."

She smiled then went into a coughing fit. Rupert lost his smile and wished he could imagine a cure.

Rupert and Squeem stood before the red door. Folky and Ensen watched Pie O'Sky's bagoon drifting away. Rupert turned to her.

"Thanks for all the fun," he said.

She smiled and gave him a hug.

"You think we'll ever see each other again?"

"I think so. Take care of your coffus."

"My what?"

"Your cough. I wish I could Imagine a way to cure it."

"I'll be fine," she insisted then whispered, "And I'll take care of the bell. Make sure no one ever finds it."

"Thanks," Rupert said. "And thank you, Mr. Ensen,"

He held out his hand. Ensen took it and shook it firmly.

"Thank *you*, Rupert. And it's Mookie. From now on, I am Mookie Starbright."

"Okay—and I'm *Rupert* Starbright."

"I will see you in your wondrous Imaginings, Rupert Starbright," Mookie said.

Rupert nodded and stepped back to the door.

"Bye, everybody," Squeem said.

"Rupert, I'll miss you!" Folky called out.

"I will never forget you, Folky!" Rupert replied. "Okay, fishkey. Open the door to Graysland."

The key floated from the chain around his neck and, like a little comet with a rainbow tail, flew into the golden keyhole.

"I'll always love you, Folky," Rupert whispered. "I mean, Grandma."

"You okay, Rupert?" Squeem asked.

"Yeah. I'll be fine. I just need to imagine one last thing before we go."

Rupert closed his eyes and let his Imagining work. When he looked again, the door stood open, and he and Squeem stepped through it. He took one last look back and watched Folky's confused face fade away.

Chapter 29

A Little Winter Joy

A river of leaves rushed down The Curving Road and around the feet of Rupert and Squeem. They looked around. The door was gone, and they stood in front of the boring houses that lined the familiar street. It would be a busy day of raking tomorrow.

"Well, we're home," Squeem said.

"Yeah. I was kind of hoping…"

"What?"

"Nothing," Rupert said with a shrug.

"Hey, what did you try to imagine? Just before we went through the door?" Squeem wanted to know.

Rupert smiled briefly before sadness filled his eyes.

"I imagined that Folky wouldn't remember my adventures with me. I imagined it would all be forgotten."

"Why?"

"Let's get home." He started down the quiet street.

They came around a bend, and Rupert stared wide-eyed. Squeem did, too.

"Do you see what I see?" he asked.

Rupert nodded. A smile spread across his face. A big happy smile.

The big bayberry tree on the lawn of 17 The Curving Road glittered in the moonlight that peeked through the clouds. Little pieces of jewelry, tinfoil, buttons and kitchen utensils hung from its branches. Standing next to the tree was his father. Their eyes met, and Rupert rushed to greet him.

"Rupert. Glad you're back. What do you think of this old tree?" Polgus said.

"I think it's the most beautiful tree I have ever seen in my life," Rupert said as tears filled his eyes.

There were tears in Polgus's eyes as well. He grabbed Rupert into a big fat bear hug.

"I figured maybe a little Winter Joy in these parts might spruce things up a bit," he said, his voice cracking with emotion.

"I think you're right, Dad."

"You wanna make sure you tell me next time you go wandering off to your imagining places?" Polgus asked.

"I will, Dad. I will."

"Hey, Squeem. Take a peek at that leaf-covered lawn of yours." Polgus said, gesturing down the road.

"Wow!"

Squeem's mother stood by a little pine she, too, had decorated. He raced off to join her.

"Rupert!"

He looked to see his mom and grandmother hurrying out of the house. He rushed over and gave his mother a hug then turned to his grandmother.

"Hi, Grandma. Isn't the Winter Joy tree great?" he said.

"It's a beauty. I always knew your father was a softy deep inside," she said. "A merry Winter's Joy to you, my dear boy."

She started coughing. Rupert's excitement turned to sadness.

"What's wrong? No sad pusses when the Winter Pussy Cat is in the sky!"

"Grandma, I wish…I wish that…"

"What, Rupert? What do you wish?"

"I wish that boy had been faster than me." Rupert said softly.

Folka's eyebrows twisted a bit as she tried to figure out what he meant.

"Did I ever tell you about one Winter Joy season when I was about your age?"

He shook his head.

"This wonderful boy visited my town. We had such amazing adventures together. There was this mean old man who wanted to put an end to the spirit of Winter Joy, but we stopped him. I wish I could remember that boy's name."

"But nobody celebrates Winter Joy anymore. So we— I mean, you didn't really stop him." Rupert desperately tried to understand how she could remember it.

"I said he tried to stop the *spirit* of Winter Joy. Rupert, seasons come and go. The leaves change colors, and the sky gets cold. People change. Towns change. Just because the sky is blue and sunny doesn't mean it forgot how to snow."

Rupert was confused by her colorful way of explaining things, but as he looked into her smiling eyes, he began to understand that the answer was really simple.

"Just because a bunch of old fuddy-duddies forgot about the spirit of Winter Joy doesn't mean we all have to," he said.

His grandmother smiled proudly.

"Exactly, Rupert. It really doesn't matter who or how many people celebrate it. All that matters is that the folks who want to…do."

She smiled wide, and her many wrinkles folded over each other. But her eyes still sparkled the way the fiery young Folky's had all those years that were just a few minutes ago.

Rupert looked at the tree and tried to silence all the questions he still had. What had happened to Mookie Starbright? Where was the big bell?

He realized he didn't care. He was happy. He was back home with his mom and dad, his grandma and his best friend, and he was standing next to the most beautiful tree he had ever seen. Even prettier than anything in the Garden of Dreams in Far-Myst.

He looked up at the two glowing eyes of Aranthal. He smiled.

Grandma's right, he thought. *It doesn't matter how many people celebrate the Winter Joy. All it takes is one person to fill that night with magic.*

END

ABOUT THE AUTHOR

MIKE DICERTO has been a filmmaker and writer since childhood. His first novel, *Milky Way Marmalade*, received rave reviews and was the winner of the 2003 Dream Realm Award.

A certified yoga instructor, Mike has many interests, including gardening (loves growing chili peppers in his rooftop garden), playing guitar (and trying hard to get better), cats (long-time volunteer at NYC's Ollie's Place Adoption Center), astronomy, quantum physics, consciousness, music, comic books and Mystery Science Theatre 3000.

He lives quite contently in a NYC apartment with his wife and soul mate Suzy and their rescued kitties, Cosmo and Rupert.

ABOUT THE ARTISTS

BRAD W. FOSTER is an illustrator, cartoonist, writer, publisher, and whatever other labels he can use to get him through the door. He's won the Fan Artist Hugo a few times, picked up a Chesley Award and turned a bit of self-publishing started more than twenty-five years ago into the Jabberwocky Graphix publishing empire. (Total number of employees: 2.) Most recently, he was named the Artist Guest of Honor for the 2015 World Science Fiction Convention.

His strange drawings and cartoons have appeared in more than two thousand publications, half of those science fiction fanzines, where he draws just for the fun of it. On a more professional level, he has worked as an illustrator for various genre magazines and publishers, including *Amazing Stories* and *Dragon*. In comics, he had his own series some years back, *The Mechthings*, and he even got to play with the "big boys" for a few years as the official "Big Background Artist" of Image Comic's *Shadowhawk*.

He is known throughout the world (although most of the world doesn't know it yet) for his intricate pen-and-ink work in places as varied as *Cat Fancy*, *Cavalier*, and *Highlights for Children*. Most recently he has completed covers for a couple of Yard Dog Press books, illustrations for magazines such as *Space & Time* and *Tale-*

bones, and illustrations for the first of Carole Nelson Douglas's Cozy Noir Press books on Midnight Louie.

He spends huge sections of the year with his lovely wife Cindy showing and selling his artwork at festivals and conventions around the country.

TAMIAN WOOD is currently based out of sunny South Florida. Using art, photography, typography and digital collage techniques, she creates book covers· that appeal to the eye and the mind, to entice the book browser to become a book reader. She holds degrees in computer science and graphic design and is a proud member of Phi Theta Kappa National Honour Society.